gold and the bear

VIVIENNE SAVAGE

Lady Victoria hungers for excitement, but how can she find it while cloistered in her cousin's castle? Encouraged to journey north to pursue an adventure of her own, an abandoned lodge seems as fine a place as any to stop for rest.

Ramsay is a shifter without a mate. Overwhelmed by the responsibilities of becoming his clan's new Father Bear—and the female attention that comes with that title—he leaves on holiday to enjoy a peaceful northern hunting lodge. Finding his bed occupied by a golden-haired beauty wasn't part of the plan, but claiming her may be.

Also By Vivienne Savage

Prologue
THREE YEARS AGO

O F ALL THE favors Lady Victoria intended to ask of her cousin, permission to part from the castle hadn't been one of them. The question suddenly welled out of her all at once, as if it had a life of its own.

Queen Anastasia stared across the round tea table. "You want to go visit the wolves again? So soon?"

"I do," Victoria replied, feeling scrutinized and under study. "Is that so strange?"

Ana sipped her tea. "Only a little. It isn't necessary to ask me permission to do what you want. I'm not your mother. Or your father, thank the stars. Uncle Humphrey is an impossible arse."

"But you rely on me to look after the little ones."

"Victoria, the children love you dearly, but I've never considered you their nurse or even a governess for that matter. They'll make do without you. How long will you be gone?"

Victoria dropped her gaze to the table and shifted in the seat, discomfort raising heat along her neck. "I don't know," she murmured. She held the crumpled note from Griogair in her hands beneath the table, read over and over since the messenger bird had brought the missive to her.

Ana set her cup aside and leaned forward. "Has Griogair begun to court you—"

"No!" Victoria exclaimed, almost tipping back the chair.

"Oh. It's just that Alistair and I had wondered a few times…"

"Ana, how could you? He's old enough to be my father. In fact, he treats me like a daughter." It wasn't that the werewolf lorekeeper wasn't handsome in his own way, but that she simply felt nothing romantic toward him.

"All right. All right. Truth be told, I had hoped you finally found someone. So, if not Griogair, is there another wolf?"

"It's nothing like that." Victoria picked at the edge of her dress sleeve. "I want to go and learn from them."

A perplexed wrinkle formed on Ana's brow. "Learn what?"

"To fight and to take care of myself." A year had passed since Maeval abducted her, but she still had awful nightmares.

"Alistair or I could teach you as much. Or even one of the guardsmen."

"You all have duties of your own and the guardsmen are busy squashing out the hidden pockets of disease in the far corners of Etherling."

"Nonsense. We'd make the time for you."

"No, because you'll always see me as your cousin first. A noblewoman. Griogair and his clan don't. They won't treat me gently because of who I am." She drew in a deep breath, knowing it was now or never. "During my last visit to see

Griogair, the wolves invited me to live among them for a while. I've accepted."

"All right."

"All right?"

"I want your happiness, and if this will bring it to you, then go with our blessing and love. Write often to Elspeth. She'll miss you."

"And I'll miss her."

One of the hardest parts of leaving was figuring out what to bring and what to leave behind. In the end, she decided to leave it all save for a few personal items. Even more difficult than choosing among her numerous belongings was wondering how much time would pass before she could return to her cousin's home with an accomplishment under her belt.

A small number of guards traveled with her to the bottom of the mountain as her personal escort, but they weren't necessary once she reached the lowest slope and found a pack of wolves awaiting her. Griogair, one of the largest and oldest among the five shifters, raised his haunches and approached her with a wolfish grin on his scarred face.

She envied the ease with which he shifted and the power he exuded even at his age. The others remained in their four-legged bodies but inclined their furry heads to her in greeting.

"You brought so many of them."

"Aye, they haven't seen Benthwaite in years and fondly remember the sweet hares that dwell at the base of the mountain. Don't mind them. Now, do you suppose that beast of yours can keep up with us?"

"Rook loves to run."

"Good."

Victoria looked forward to the ride and the tranquil nights beneath the stars. While sleeping outside would be new to her, she'd decided no discomfort would ever surpass the imprisonment she'd endured as Maeval's slave and source of energy.

Griogair couldn't communicate with her as a wolf, but he jogged alongside her on his long, lean legs, in good shape despite his age. She'd asked once, beyond curious to know, and she couldn't believe he was nearing eighty, despite the gray streaks in his dark beard.

Sometimes, desiring conversation or intuitive enough to realize Victoria desired a chat, Griogair transformed and walked beside Rook. But no matter how often she rode in silence, the time on the road never dragged.

There was something beautiful and peaceful about those nights with the wolves.

Victoria knew they were at the edge of the Misty Woods, which the pack called home, when she recognized the gentle fog sweeping in on the fourth night. Although he'd never admit it and wanted to spare her pride, she knew the old wolf took his time because of her.

Everything ached. And there'd be no hot soaks in a porcelain tub for her once she reached their camp.

"It isn't necessary to stop so often, Griogair," she told him.

The big wolf transformed mid-step. "Who says we're stopping for you?" He grinned.

While the immense werewolves were prone to moments of showing off, chasing each other, and racing across the green lowlands, they also took frequent breaks to hunt in the brush. Griogair had claimed it was normal behavior for boys.

Less than an hour later, as she was laying out her bedroll and removing supplies from her saddlebags, one of those "boys" brought her a long-eared hare as a courtship offering, shifting to two legs and standing beside Rook while very naked, and very, very interested in Victoria. She flushed so hard she thought her hair would ignite and catch fire.

"You said they were boys," she hissed at Griogair when the wolf returned from scouting ahead.

"Isn't that what they are?"

She stared at her friend. "Certainly not."

He chuckled at her. "I may have neglected to mention a few are interested in you, Goldilocks. Think nothing of it."

"I realized that when he came at me with his dead rabbit," she muttered. "Not that I don't appreciate the offer, but I…"

"What is it?" Griogair coaxed gently when she hesitated to continue. "What do you want, lass?"

What did she want? Less than eight years ago, she'd been young and eager to marry, looking forward to the usual ritual of meeting young men chosen by her parents. And when every attempt to marry had fallen through, she'd remained home, a spinster, until her dear cousin paid the bride-price demanded by her parents and brought her home to Benthwaite.

"I don't believe I am capable of being a wife to anyone right now," she said in a quiet voice. "I'm weak, and I'm useless. I can't catch my own food. I'm good for nothing at all but knitting doilies and cross-stitching flowers. Why should any of them want me?"

"You're a beautiful woman."

"I want to be more than that," she said, plucking petals off a wildflower. "I want someone who wants me for more than my pretty face or my title."

"You know titles mean nothing here, especially those from Creag Morden. You made a nice impression on them when you last visited, Victoria, and the lads are showing genuine interest—but if you're not ready, that's your choice to make."

"No one will be upset?"

"No. It's not our way to force anyone. But Victoria"—he shifted closer and tipped her face up—"what is it you truly want?"

"I never want to feel such helplessness again, but I don't know where to begin. What if I'm too weak to—"

"You certainly aren't weak, my girl. Far from it. There's no weakness in realizing one's own flaws and fighting to overcome them."

"My flaws? Everything about me is a flaw. I'm only human and nothing special among them, with exception of a meaningless title. I don't have Anastasia's magic, or Alistair's shifting ability. I'll never be like you and Conall."

"And you need not be like us. There's a strength in being who you are," Griogair insisted. "Listen to me, lass. You need not have huge teeth and fangs to bring down your prey. You'll learn to fight. I promise."

Through her tears, she nodded and swallowed the tension gripping her throat.

Griogair was right. She wasn't weak, after all. And with his tutelage, she'd never allow anyone to hurt her again.

Chapter 1

W HAT KIND OF Father Bear could he possibly be when he had no mate or young of his own? The question haunted Ramsay as he trudged through the forest and overgrown brambles toward their hunting lodge carrying a net swollen with fish.

At the behest of his fellow leaders in the clan, he'd taken a necessary sanity break from the overwhelming duties of leading his household. He'd caved to the pressure, packed a single bag, and made the ten-day trip to their cabin on the borders of Creag Morden and Cairn Ocland. The thick forest on the northern side of the mountains had been unclaimed territory when the bears first built their lodge six generations ago. The neighboring kingdom of Creag Morden had expanded their reach since then.

He enjoyed three days of peace and quiet, and grudgingly admitted to himself the break was a good idea. Even if it was a bit lonely. Talbot and Heldreth were due to join him today, so he had spent hours by the creekside with a fishing pole and net while gathering enough sustenance to feed the other two bears once they arrived.

Clan Ardal, the bear shifters of Cairn Ocland, consisted

of three noble families and many more common bears. Only a year ago, he'd been known as Little Bear, a voice for all youth of the clan, but as a man of thirty-eight, he wasn't quite so little a bear anymore.

Despite his better intentions of claiming a mate, none of the women of Clan Ardal interested him. He'd met the courageous and the bold, the sweet and the dainty, skilled artisans, capable brawlers, and the best chefs in their village, but none were the woman for him. Ramsay wanted a woman whose traits encompassed the best of everything. Wit, ferocity, loyalty, and beauty wrapped into a fine mate able to hold her own against him.

Perhaps Heldreth was right, and his fantasies had created a perfect, nonexistent woman.

Upon reaching the lodge, he dropped his bounty of fish on the porch and pulled up a stool. Using a bucket to catch the refuse, he expertly scaled and cleaned a dozen of the slippery perch. He harvested the abundant herbs in the overgrown garden and reclaimed vegetables from the wilderness. At the edge of the same lake where he'd acquired the fish, he found enough water chestnuts to accompany the soup.

He read while the stew bubbled and became lost in one of the Mordenian romances Heldreth kept on the shelf. Novels from the kingdom of Creag Morden tended to be heavy on love, passion, and wit.

While he'd never admit to liking them, he owned several at home.

"The humans aren't so different from us, after all," he muttered. "Except for their primitive views toward courtship."

There wasn't an Oclander woman alive who would obediently accept her father choosing a husband for her. While she would tolerate his suggestions, a man who respected his daughter would never treat her akin to property.

And when he finally had a daughter of his own one day, he'd be sure to impress upon her the importance of always following her heart and speaking her mind, even to him.

One day.

Until then, Ramsay would entertain one unsuitable prospect after the next in hopes of one day encountering his ideal mate.

Soon the hours passed from afternoon to evening, and a storm swept in from the east. He watched the darkening clouds thicken across what had been a serene, perfect sky, and stood from his chair. He ladled generous bowls of stew and placed them over enchanted warming stones on the table. Afterward, he spiced Talbot's food to lethal levels of heat while wondering how his friend could tolerate so much pepper.

Making three individual bowls to their specific tastes wasn't hard when Heldreth preferred her soups bland, and once he finished stirring garlic, salt, and a little rosemary into his bowl, he returned outside.

By the time his friends arrived, the flavors would be perfect.

Just as he sat down to resume a particularly spicy love

Goldilocks & the Bear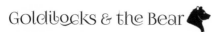

scene in his novel, an eagle landed beside him on the wooden rail. The enormous bird wore a leather case fastened to its leg, the variety used for messenger and carrier birds preferred by the clans. Curious, he spilled the note from the case and unraveled it.

Heldreth and Talbot had canceled their plans to meet him for the gathering. Apparently, they'd encountered a royal messenger beseeching the bear clan's aid in Etherling. The king and queen had finally decided to retake the city from the wilderness. There, they would work alongside the monarchs as they rebuilt the city stone by stone.

Their hopes were for Ramsay to enjoy his break away from his responsibilities in their honor.

Worry not for us, Little Bear wrote in his cramped and squished scrawl. *There are many beautiful huntresses here of the human persuasion, and I look forward to making their acquaintance. There will be another time to take our holiday with you at the lodge.*

With great fondness,
Talbot and Heldreth

Blast. Groaning, Ramsay glanced back through the open door at the three servings and enormous pot of remaining stew on the stove. With no one else to partake, most of his efforts would go to waste. If he'd known, he would have hunted instead and salted the excess meat.

As there was no sense in crying over spilled milk, he scribed a brief letter of acknowledgment and sent the bird back to the south. As he did, thunder boomed in the distance, the herald of an approaching storm.

Damn. Double unlucky.

"C'mon now, lad," Ramsay said to Dunn, the handsome but stocky horse he'd been riding for the past ten years. The stallion had grazed nearby for most of the day, a placid companion while Ramsay read. Despite his great girth and size, he was no braver than a finch. "Let's get you put away safely before the storm strikes."

Rain poured at once. The skies opened and released a bounty of warm summer rain, and while it felt good against his skin, his skittish friend pranced in place.

"It's only rain. You know that."

Ramsay stepped down from the porch. Upon reaching the stallion, the beast danced away.

"Now stop that. This isn't the time to—"

Lightning blinded him when a bolt fell from the sky and struck a branch from the tree mere yards away from them. It fell with a startling crash to the ground. The boom deafened Ramsay and reduced his steed to mindless terror.

The horse bolted.

"Dunn!" Ramsay bellowed beneath the turbulent skies, but it was no good. The horse galloped away without looking back. Given no alternative, Ramsay snatched a length of rope from the porch and charged into the rain behind him.

Victoria had never enjoyed her own adventure before. She'd heard tales from others and experienced a terrifying abduction, but she'd never been the heroine of her very own story. After two years with the wolves and another back at Castle TalDrach since her return from the pack, she couldn't wait to set out on her own. To go home and show her parents the woman she had become.

It's only a silly ride home to Creag Morden. Nothing adventurous about that, she thought.

But it was more than she'd ever undertaken before. With only a temporary magical spell to hasten her journey from the neighboring kingdom of Cairn Ocland, she'd taken the northern mountain pass through the once uninhabited goblin mines. Thanks to Princess Teagan, the foul little creatures associated with humankind again.

It's wrong to call them foul, she thought, chastising herself. They deserved more than that for the role they'd played in restoring peace to the kingdom.

While her thoughts wandered, a stray raindrop fell upon her nose. The skies had taken on a stormy, overcast look, and a single drop meant more was soon to come. Most of her trip over the past few days had been through fair weather, so of course, it was only natural that a storm should eventually sweep in.

  VIVIENNE SAVAGE

And now wasn't the time to panic over a few raindrops, not when it had taken her days to convince Anastasia that she could make it home without an escort of armed guards.

Braced for the inevitable onslaught, Victoria continued down the lane, exhausted from a day of riding but prepared for the oncoming storm.

"Looks like rain, Rook. We're going to get drenched if we don't find shelter soon, but we'll survive, won't we?"

The gelding snorted and picked up his pace to a trot. He didn't like getting wet any more than Victoria did, the spoiled creature.

Her map didn't show a village for miles, but she noticed a narrow path leading off the main road. Victoria could only hope it led to someone's home or farm.

With no other idea where to go, she guided Rook onto the hard-packed trail. It cut through the trees on a straight course without any turns, eventually widening enough that the branches no longer scraped at her sides.

She almost didn't see the cabin at first because, while it was large, it was recessed a good distance of over a hundred yards away from the path and the trees were so thick the setting sun dimmed her view of the meadow clearing.

A thunderclap boomed overhead. Rook reared up on his hind legs, nearly throwing her from the saddle, and twisted around. He bolted toward the cabin and directly into a three-horse stable built against it. More thunder rumbled across the darkening sky, preceded by a bright flash. Victoria stared outside with wide eyes. The storm had come faster than she'd expected. That or her weather sense was abysmal. She hated to admit it was likely the latter.

"It's okay, boy." She patted Rook's neck then slid down from his back. She removed his saddle and slung it onto the stone-carved rack. A year ago, she'd lacked the muscle to accomplish such a feat without strain. It came easily now. "It's okay. We'll stay the night here."

Someone had to be home, judging by the fresh hay and oats set out. She spent a few minutes calming her horse and removing his remaining tack while the skies split open and released a heavy downpour. Victoria prepared herself then dashed through the rain. She crashed into the cabin door and shoved it open.

"Please forgive me for barging in!" she cried as she used her body to slam the door shut against the wind.

No one answered.

Pushing her wet hair back from her face, Victoria stared into an empty room. Water dripped from her cloak onto the polished wooden floors.

"Hello?" she called again.

A low fire burned in an oversized hearth across the room. The welcoming warmth beckoned her, but the mud on her boots and drenched clothes kept her lingering near the door.

Should she go in and help herself? Where were the people who lived here?

The next ground-shaking boom made the decision

for Victoria, her mind made up as the intolerable weather worsened. Nothing could make her go back out into the storm unless she discovered her host was an ax murderer.

She tugged off her boots and set them to the side, then wrung out her cloak as best she could before hanging it on a conveniently placed peg. She ventured farther inside. It appeared to be a single large room with tanned skins stretched between posts, several used as portable walls. A peek behind one divider revealed a row of three tidy beds, all in differing sizes.

Although no one was present, the cabin had to have an owner. Perhaps the poor soul had been trapped in a dry place to hide from the rain.

In the kitchen to her left, she saw a long counter beside a circular table topped with three steaming bowls and three heavy mugs. Following her rumbling tummy, she stepped over to the table, and the aroma of fish stew cramped her stomach with hunger.

"I wonder if they'd mind me helping myself to some food." Surely with such a warm bounty, they wouldn't mind. Would they? She spied a pot on the stove but not a single bowl in the doorless cupboards. Only the three on the table.

"I'll eat one of these, wash the bowl, and refill it," she decided after her stomach made another embarrassing noise.

Red flecks floated on the surface of the first soup bowl, each pepper flake glittering like garnet chips in the golden broth. Victoria leaned down for a cautious sniff. While it didn't smell too spicy, a small taste proved otherwise. Heat exploded across her tongue, burned up her nostrils, and made her eyes water.

She didn't care what was in the nearby mug, so long as it quenched the fire in her mouth. "Who can eat food that spicy?"

A dragon probably. Alistair would have swallowed the entire thing down without a complaint. And maybe Anastasia too, but her cousin had always been the braver one.

The thick, dark ale wasn't so bad and it helped temper the heat in her mouth. Moving to the next bowl, she leaned above it and inhaled. It smelled of only fish, making her crinkle her nose. It looked unappealing by comparison.

Bypassing the second and moving to the third bowl, Victoria gazed at the contents with hopeful eyes. "Maybe the third time will be a charm," she muttered, distrusting the potentially bland dish and tasting the third. It was. Delicious flavors of garlic and herbs exploded against her tongue, seasoned to perfection with the ideal amount of salt and flavor from the fish.

"I've invaded their home and stolen someone's food," she muttered, only to sigh with disdain for herself. Ana would say she was definitely not ready for an adventure.

Once she'd eaten, she rinsed the bowl and replaced its contents with the unseasoned stew over the stove. Hopefully her unwitting host would understand. To make amends, she straightened the kitchen, washed the knives and preparation tools, and wiped bits of chopped herbs from the counters. She even swept the floors.

Outside, the rain pounded against the roof as though stones were falling from the sky. Uninvited or not, she couldn't go back out into that.

As exhaustion took its toll from her journey and cleaning the mystery homeowner's kitchen, she wandered past the partition. Hoping one or more of the beds were purely for guests, and promising to leave gold behind in the morning if the occupants didn't return, Victoria sat on the edge of the closest bed.

And sank into its pillowy top. It swallowed her like a cloud until she struggled out of it, for a moment fearing she'd wandered into—or quite literally laid in—some forest witch's trap.

Wouldn't that be a way to die? She could hear Anastasia already, admonishing her in death for landing in some hag's oven. Her imprint remained when she glanced back at the bed.

"Well, that won't do."

The next bed didn't give under her weight at all and had to be the most uncomfortable mattress she'd ever found. And she'd slept in a wolf's den with only a blanket on the rocky floor.

"This bed is as hard as a stone slab," Victoria muttered.

Skeptical of this strange cabin she'd found deep in the woods, she squinted at the third bed. If the first was too soft, and the second too hard, then certainly the third would be just right. Tentatively, she settled on the edge and wiggled to test it. Overcome with relief, she collapsed backward onto the mattress with her arms spread at her sides. Perfect.

Ramsay trudged through the rain with his head down and his horse trailing behind him. After a two-hour chase through the storm, all he wanted was a hot meal and a dry bed.

"In you go, you scaredy-cat," he grumbled at the stallion. "No more running—" He drew to a halt and stared at the unfamiliar horse occupying the second stall of the stable. "Huh. Maybe the others changed their minds after all."

He wondered if they had some bigger joke planned. He wouldn't put it past the bear matron.

After securing the stable, he headed inside and kicked off his boots. It didn't take long to notice the changes around the place. A pair of boots, too small to belong to any bear he knew, sat beside the door. The floors had been swept and wood added to the hearth.

Heldreth never cleaned up after him, and Talbot was a perpetual slob.

He stripped down to his smallclothes and tossed the soaked garments near the fire, loathing trousers but of the mind to dress as the natives of Creag Morden during his travels through their kingdom. Pants hadn't yet taken Cairn Ocland fashion by storm, the style worn mostly by farmers and young women. Men of the traditional clans clung tenaciously to their

VIVIENNE SAVAGE

kilts, and Ramsay would forever remain one of them while at home.

Since his housemaid had yet to appear, he would unravel that mystery come first light. He was too tired to care otherwise.

With the hearth nearby, he quickly warmed while wolfing down his portion of the stew, although he was startled to find it bland. He put two and two together, realizing his uninvited visitor must have been starved.

Ramsay snorted, unable to blame his guest for bypassing the other two bowls. After wolfing down his portion and Heldreth's serving, he made his way into the bedroom. It wasn't until he reached for his blankets that he noticed the golden head peeking out from beneath the covers.

Had they sent him entertainment instead, deciding the best way to coerce their new Father Bear into a vacation would be for him to take his comfort in a soft woman? The plan seemed devious enough for Little Bear, with a hint of Heldreth's busybody nature. Hadn't she been the one to suggest for him to claim a mate and do it soon?

Ramsay grunted. Had the others not preferred their beds to be unsuitable polar opposites, he would have crawled into one of them instead. For a moment, he didn't know what to do, confused by the girl's presence. She didn't smell like bear or have the broad shoulders and muscular physique of a shifter woman.

Peeling back the blankets for a look at her confirmed his suspicions. Her slight frame, fragile and fine-boned, would have broken beneath a bear woman's fists. Her blonde hair spilled as gold as the sun over his pillows, and freckles stood out against her fair cheeks.

Not knowing what to make of it, he admired her longer. The fact that she'd chosen his bed couldn't be a coincidence, so he threw caution to the wind and crawled in beneath the blankets.

Her hair smelled like lilacs, and when he curled his arms around her, she snuggled in closer against him. While she'd gone to bed in too much clothing—her simple nightshift interrupting the skin-to-skin contact he would have preferred—she was still an improvement over sleeping alone. He nuzzled her once or twice but found her sound asleep, unresponsive aside from a content, indiscernible murmur.

The peaceful rhythm of her breathing lulled him to sleep. With his arms around her, he held her safe and secure.

An explosion of pain in the abdomen jerked Ramsay awake. He tumbled back and out of the large bed, landing on the wooden floor.

Ramsay's mind jumped to a dozen possibilities, the worst of them being that they were under attack. He got his bearings and prepared to shift, leaping to his feet before he realized the girl was crouched above him on the bed with a dagger in her hand and fire in her eyes.

"What in the stars was that about?" he roared. The pain rapidly faded, but the bewilderment only worsened with each passing second.

"Who are you?" his assailant questioned in his language, her Oclander flawed but understandable. "How dare you welcome yourself to my bed as if I were some strumpet to be fondled in sleep?"

"*Your* bed?" he growled low, the noise rumbling through his chest. "You invade *my* lodge and *my* bed, then have the sheer cheek to pull a knife on me?"

"Do you often crawl into bed with strangers?"

"When I'm tired and want my bed, yes," he snapped back. When he moved closer, the girl feinted with the blade and warned him back again. It made him want her even more. For a human, she had nerve. A spine of steel, something he wouldn't have expected of a fragile non-shifter. "Come back to bed with me."

"No. In fact, I think I'll be leaving."

Thunder cracked overhead and shook the cabin, making them both glance toward the nearest window. Another booming roll soon followed.

"You won't be going anywhere in this weather. Now, who sent you, girl? Was it Talbot?"

Her brow creased. "No one sent me here at all."

Studying her long enough to take in her state of partial undress, his eyes swept the dimmed room until he located travel leathers and a cloak. "So you're an intruder who chose to help herself to my lodge."

"I didn't mean to," she said in a more apologetic tone. "In fact, I'd planned to beg your kindness to escape the storm."

"But I wasn't here."

The knife wavered and lowered an inch as indecision furrowed her brow again. "I will leave if I must. Putting you out wasn't my intention."

Ramsay ran his fingers through his short blond hair. A beautiful woman had landed in his lap by chance, and she couldn't wait to be away from him. "You haven't put me out. If you must know, I'd expected the company of my fellow clansmen, who won't be joining me after all. I'd say help yourself to my lodgings, but you've already done that."

Hot color spread across her cheeks. "I planned to leave some coins if no one showed up before I left, and I did clean up my mess." Her gaze drifted lower and passed over his chest, only to jerk upward again to his face.

"Coin isn't necessary. I've plenty of my own. Ah… listen. Stay the night then, and we'll call this a misunderstanding. The storm is raging out there, and your poor horse doesn't deserve the punishment." He gestured to the bed. "Go on then."

She hesitated. "Since this is your bed, I'll sleep in another."

"No, it's fine. You crawl back in, and I'll take Heldreth's. How she sleeps in that cloud, I'll never know, but it's better than Talbot's rock."

"Heldreth? Of Clan Ardal?"

He blinked at her in surprise. Although they had built their lodge years ago, before he'd first taken the role of Little Bear, he'd never met anyone in Creag Morden familiar with his people. When his predecessor chose their land just beyond the Cairn Ocland border, they'd placed it in contested territory and left fae charms surrounding it.

By all rights, the blonde waif should never have found it. Curiouser and curiouser, he studied his unexpected houseguest. "Yes. Do you know her?"

"Somewhat. We met a few years ago, at Mount Kinros. My cousin introduced us."

His brows shot up again. The only people at Mount Kinros had been in battle, and while fierce, she hardly looked like a warrior. He'd have remembered meeting her.

"Are you one of the huntresses then? I don't recall fighting alongside you. What's your name?"

"Victoria."

Ramsay's breath stilled in his chest. Victoria had come a long way from being the traumatized, weeping girl in his memories. He recalled a thin and frail doll with scarcely any meat at all on her. While she'd retained her slender figure, she'd picked up enough weight to be attractive, and there was now warmth in her cheeks and life in her eyes.

"I met you, though you were in poor condition for an introduction."

"Nonsense. I would remember you."

The corner of his mouth rose. "I was in a different form then. One too large to fit in this room. I'm Ramsay."

Her lips formed a small circle. "Oh!" Then her gaze dropped to the state of her garments, and she squeaked before leaping behind one of the large dividers. "I'm not dressed!"

"Lass, if there's anything to see, I've been looking at it for the past five minutes of our conversation," he said in a patient voice.

"I…" Coerced by the sense in his words, she emerged again. The color remained on her freckled cheeks. "It isn't appropriate."

"Neither is entering a stranger's home unannounced and without permission, but as you were fine with that, save yourself and that horse an awful night. You did clean up my mess after all. I'll consider us even."

As the tension between them faded, Victoria lowered her guard. "All right."

"Good. As I said, take my bed for the eve." Contrary to Heldreth's frequent teasing, he could be a gentleman when he desired to be, when the moment suited him, and at this moment, impressing upon Victoria that he wouldn't harm her took precedence over a comfortable night on his own mattress.

Even if he would prefer sleeping beside her instead.

Chapter 2

VICTORIA AWAKENED TO the aroma of cooking meat and additional weight on her body. Ramsay must have tossed another blanket over her in the middle of the night, and its hide reminded her of silk. For a while, the aches and pains of travel convinced her to remain beneath it.

Creag Morden's unpredictable weather patterns could pound punishing showers and freezing hail one morning, and shine bright hours later by afternoon. Spending the past seven years in Cairn Ocland had been a pleasant difference and introduction to a reasonable climate.

And for some reason, she'd voluntarily undertaken the journey back north. She shivered under the blankets and dreaded slipping from beneath them. Her dagger remained where she'd left it, her fingers grazing the handle without wrapping around it. A glance at the two adjacent beds showed only tidy blankets and no sign of Ramsay.

"Are you awake yet?" he called in his rumbling voice. He spoke as she'd expect a bear to sound if given words, all bass and masculinity.

Please, if there are gods at all, let this man have put on clothing. Because she didn't know if she could tolerate another moment of gazing upon him in only his undergarments. On Ramsay, smallclothes were truly small, revealing the definition of his thighs and the leanness of his hips. He wasn't slim and lithe, like some of the wolf shifters she'd met. Instead, his body had been composed of sturdy limbs, broad shoulders, and a neck thick as a tree trunk. And then there were the tattoos. Green and silver ink twined down his arm in a pattern similar to the tartan kilts worn by the men of Cairn Ocland.

How in the world had she gazed upon the man and maintained a straight face while holding him at knifepoint? He'd been the finest example of masculinity, with such broad shoulders and biceps thicker than her thighs. Soft golden hairs had dusted his chest, and she'd ached to touch it and drag her fingers through them.

Above all of that, she'd been more taken by his eyes. They were dark but welcoming, a warm shade of brown turned amber in the light of the flames from the hearth. The enormous hide sheets strung up to separate the open social quarters from the private bedroom hadn't completely dimmed the area. She'd seen enough to haunt her thoughts forever.

"Ramsay?" Her hoarse voice made her cringe.

"Good morning," he called back to her.

Victoria tossed the covers off and set her bare feet on the chilly floor. "Good morning." She came from behind the divider to find him setting the table. He'd already donned trousers but walked barefoot across the floor. The bowls of fish stew had been removed, and in their place, she saw the largest breakfast she could never eat in a single sitting.

Her knees trembled. She told herself the weakness was from hunger—for food, not Ramsay's body. "Is that for me?"

He glanced up at her and his warm brown eyes crinkled at the corners. "Well, it certainly isn't for your stallion. Come over and fill your belly, lass." He set down a steaming mug beside her meal with more tea than she usually drank in a sitting. Refusing to look a gift horse in the mouth, she hurried to the chair.

"Thank you." The carved wood plate held a bounty of beans and two soft eggs. She bit into the crisp sausage and released the most inappropriate groan of pleasure.

Ramsay chuckled. "I'll take it that means my cooking is to your satisfaction."

Unable to speak with a full mouth, Victoria bobbed her head in agreement then washed it down with the fragrant tea. Although she'd expected something ultra-masculine and earthy, it smelled like jasmine and cherries.

"The rain is still coming down hard. You're welcome to stay until it lets up." Ramsay pushed a bowl toward her. She glanced down at the generous serving of hot porridge sprinkled with nuts and honey drizzles. How was she to make room for everything?

Somehow she did. What had been a meal large enough for two people fit with room to spare in her belly. Ramsay watched her, brows raised.

"What?" she asked when she couldn't take it anymore.

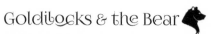

"You're not how I imagined. You even drew a knife on me last eve. Where did a noblewoman learn to wield a blade? Did King Alistair teach you?"

She shook her head. "No, though he's encouraged my training."

"The queen then. I suppose I should have expected as much. She's a fierce woman for a human."

"No, Ana had no hand in it either. I learned from the wolves. Griogair taught me."

Ramsay's brows drew together. "Ah, I see. So you've taken a mate from Clan TalWolthe."

The absurd notion made her sputter. She raised a napkin to her lips and forced down her mouthful before she could choke on it. Her vision blurred with tears and she coughed, clearing her throat. "What? No!"

"Ah. My mistake."

"Why would you think that?"

"Why else would a man take a woman under his wing and teach her?"

"To be friends," she gritted out. "Are you to tell me that the men of your bear clan are so short-sighted and selfish they'll only help a woman if it gets them in her knickers?" Once the uncouth words began to fly from her mouth, there was no stopping them. No bringing them back.

"I…" Ramsay grunted and turned his attention to his eggs and porridge. He didn't speak for a while, and they dined in silence until he finally offered, "Perhaps I chose my words poorly, Victoria. I meant, there are few shifters, male or female, willing to dedicate their time to guiding someone who isn't of personal relationship to them. You're not a member of their clan, so I assumed you to be his mate."

"Griogair is like a father to me… We… We shared a traumatic experience and became good friends. I'd trust him with my life." Ramsay's eyes reminded her of warm fire brandy, the golden brown of polished amber. After a while of eye contact between them, she looked away and cleared her throat. "Anyway, he's taught me how to handle myself."

"That's good. Then tell me, what's drawn you away from Benthwaite?"

"I'm going home for a visit to Lorehaven. It's been ages since I've seen my family, and I miss them."

"You could have been there by dragonback in a day."

"I know, but…" She caught her lip between her teeth and looked away.

"But…?" he prodded.

"I wanted to do it on my own. To show that I don't need them to coddle me anymore." Her gaze drifted to the window and the storm outside. "I'm not off to a good start, am I?"

"Oh, I wouldn't say that. You found shelter."

"Broke in, you mean."

"You found food."

"Ate yours."

Ramsay's deep chuckle brushed against her senses like a caress. It sent a shiver trickling down her spine and raised the hairs on her nape. "Still, it shows you have survival skills, and better to take refuge than to die in the cold and rain. Now, how much farther is it to your Lorehaven?"

"Two weeks or more of hard riding. Why?"

"There's been bandits on the northern road. I overheard some hunters speaking of them."

"I can handle a few bandits. Besides, I have nothing of real value." She hadn't brought anything she'd mourn losing and had only enough coin to sustain herself at an inn when she crossed one.

"A pretty woman like yourself is valuable enough. More, since they'll smell the nobility on you."

She scoffed but didn't dismiss him entirely. "Well, I'll be careful then and avoid them."

"You won't have to. I'll accompany you to the city walls."

The unexpected offer took her by surprise. "Why would you do that?"

"I won't be the one to tell our king and queen—*especially* our queen—that I let you get yourself killed on the road. She'd have my pelt on her floor."

"Oh," she said in a small voice. A disturbing flicker of disappointment seeped through her, startling her as much as his escort offer. "Well, you don't have to. I'm quite capable of riding home alone. You can enjoy your… retreat."

"I said I'm going, lass, and that's final. Now, I'm going to go out to enjoy this fishing weather. Any preferences for your dinner?"

  VIVIENNE SAVAGE

"But it's pouring rain."

Ramsay flashed her a wide grin. "It might make things a bit trickier to catch, but that's half the fun." He laced his boots and disappeared into the gray morning as a gentle rain continued to drizzle over the forest.

With little else to do, Victoria helped herself to the kitchen and dirty dishes. She donned her cloak then disposed of the slop, leaving it to the scavengers outside. She scrubbed dishes, and again wiped counters, amused with how easily she'd taken to doing menial tasks.

Ten years ago, she'd have never picked up a soiled dish to wash it, and now, helping others had become second nature. Once she'd tidied the kitchen, she tested the trio of chairs by the hearth—again, she had choices equal to clouds, stone, or comfort—and recognized Ramsay's seat within moments of settling in it.

A knock stirred her from her drowsing state. At first, she thought it was a branch hitting against a wall, but then a frail voice called for help.

"What the—" Victoria scurried to the door and unlatched it. A hard gust blew the door open and a hunched figure stumbled forward, straight into her arms.

"Bless you, child," the figure wheezed. "Bless you."

"Come, let's get you near the fire."

Victoria helped the woman strip out of her dripping cloak and into a chair before rushing back to secure the door. She struggled against it at first, grateful for the momentary reprieve in the wind that let her close it. Hopefully, Ramsay was weathering the storm during his hunt.

Door secured, she hurried to the stove and poured hot tea from the kettle into a clean mug, then crossed back over to her unexpected visitor.

"Here, drink this. It'll warm you up."

"Thank you, my dear. So kind."

While the woman was old and quite shriveled, it didn't take much of Victoria's imagination to believe she'd once been beautiful. Even stunning. Age hadn't clouded her violet eyes, but her hair fell stark gray as steel down her back. Only wrinkles marred her unblemished, tanned skin, and her strange garments reminded Victoria of the robes worn by the mages who trained at the Collegium of Arthras in northern Creag Morden.

"Look at you. You're soaked." Victoria settled a heavy woolen blanket around her shoulders then followed it with a warm fur. "Where did you come from? Your accent is quite different." In her time of living in Cairn Ocland, she'd become accustomed to their lyrical cadence and the beautiful way they spoke her native language. She'd never questioned why all of them seemed versed in the Mordenian tongue.

"I've come a long, long way, child." The woman coughed and pulled the blanket tighter around herself. "My name is Safiyya. Thank you for letting me inside your home."

"And I'm Victoria. The man who owns this cabin is called Ramsay."

"Your husband?"

Victoria chuckled. "No. Like you, I sought shelter from the storm and found this place. Ramsay's been kind enough not to turn me out. Are you alone?"

Safiyya nodded and raised the hot mug of tea to her lips again. Her trembling had yet to subside. Worried for the state of the woman's horse, Victoria hurried to the door and stepped outside. Only Rook and Ramsay's stallion occupied the stable built against the cabin.

When she glanced behind her again, the old woman had drifted to sleep, still cradling the hot mug.

How in the stars had she come to them on foot?

Chapter 3

RAMSAY HADN'T BEEN exaggerating when he told Victoria the storm would make fishing a challenge, but compared to resisting her, it was easy. He'd never met a human woman who captivated him beyond her physical appearance, and he wondered how well she would have fared with her blade, had she been forced to use it.

He'd have to test her, perhaps in a little spar, to see how well Griogair had trained his young protégé.

With all the small critters hiding safely in their dens, he turned to the river. At least he knew where the fish retreated during rough waters, and his paws worked better than any net. He found a single fat and sassy salmon then caught two more smaller morsels, perfect for his guest's healthy appetite. He grinned. He'd expected her to eat like a dainty human, only for her to put away enough food to put him to shame.

Of all the women to wander into his lonely life, it had to be the cousin of the queen. That alone put her firmly off-limits. Still, he couldn't get the memory of her body curled against his chest out of his mind.

He'd better get it out of his mind, because as far as he knew, the queen's cousin wasn't on the market. They'd probably already begun the search for her mate. Even if he did qualify as nobility among the shifters, he doubted the king and queen had even taken the bears into consideration.

Everyone knew the TalDrachs preferred the cunning wolves and stately griffins.

Becoming human again, he traded paws for hands. The rain had let up to a placid mist at last, allowing him to make the hour-long trek back to the cabin without rushing. He tossed the net of fish aside on the porch and pushed open the door.

"I hope you like fish. We have plenty—" He paused, blinking at the stranger in his chair. "—of it... Hello."

"You must be Ramsay." The old woman struggled to sit up.

He shook his head and spread both of his hands, palms out toward her. "No need for that. You look like you need the rest."

"You're back." Victoria beamed at him from the stove. "I'm making honey biscuits. I hope you don't mind."

"No, not at all. I'll..." He looked between the two women and furrowed his brow. Had Victoria traveled in company after all? If so, where had she hidden the old woman overnight?

"This is Safiyya," Victoria said. "She sought shelter from the storm while you were gone."

"Ah," he said. It would take a heartless man to throw an old woman into the cold, so he relented, after releasing a heavy, pent-up breath of resignation. "I'll go clean the fish outside. The storm is letting up and should pass soon."

That was two people now who had bypassed the cabin's protections. He'd have to ask their queen if she could check on the enchantments. Perhaps time had weakened them.

After taking care of the fish, he returned inside to the sweet aroma of baking bread. Victoria and Safiyya sat at the table with tea. A third mug waited for him.

"Thank you for taking me in," Safiyya began. "Your kindness will not be forgotten."

He managed a tight smile as he took his seat. So far, his quiet retreat had turned into anything but. "If you don't mind me asking, where did you come from? It's been storming for days."

"Yes, I know. It caught up to me as I travelled the mountain pass."

Victoria startled. "You mean you came from Cairn Ocland?"

"Yes, and no. I passed through the highlands only, but I come from Samahara."

Ramsay stared at her, incredulity raising his voice in pitch. "Alone?"

The woman raised her chin, proud despite her age. "Yes. I come alone, and perhaps it's taken me quite a while to reach this far, but I will continue. Thank you for your hospitality, young man."

"Surely not without proper rest," Victoria blurted out. "You were frozen through. Where is your destination? Perhaps I could help."

Safiyya hesitated. "I'm trying to reclaim something taken from me."

"What could be so valuable you would cross multiple kingdoms to retrieve it?" Victoria asked. Ramsay wondered the same.

"A family heirloom of vast importance to me. One worth dying for if it should come to it." Despite her creaking limbs and shaky legs, Safiyya set aside her mug and rose from the seat. "And it's time that I move on now that the storm has passed."

"Wait," Victoria said. "Where was it taken? And by whom?"

"A fearsome and clever bandit called Aladdin, and I believe his stronghold is in Northern Creag Morden."

"Then I'll travel with you to Lorehaven," Victoria said.

"Oh, I couldn't do that to you, dear."

"It's no trouble, truly. Lorehaven was my destination to begin with, and I'm sure I could ask my aunt and uncle if they know anything about this bandit. But it's a long journey. We can leave tomorrow after you've had a good night's rest."

Ramsay waited until the old woman fell asleep before he dragged Victoria outside the cabin. The rain had stopped and the wind stilled. Branches lay strewn across the overgrown stone path leading to the road, blown from their trees during the storm.

Once he shut the door, Victoria snatched her arm away

Goldilocks & the Bear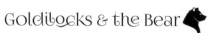

from his grip. "Must you drag me about like a barbarian?"

"What in the blazes do you think you're doing?" he demanded.

"Preparing to resume my journey north. What else would I be doing?"

"Why did you invite that old woman along with us?"

"Us? I didn't invite her to come with *us*. I invited her to come with *me*."

Ramsay pressed his lips together in a hard line. "I told you it's not safe. I'll escort you to your city and that is that. As for the old woman, you don't know her intentions or what she's—"

"I don't know you either," came the prompt retort.

Blast. She had him there. "You knew me well enough to eat my food and sleep in my bed. But have I done anything to harm you?"

"No, not yet anyway. How am I to know you're not some bad man in disguise waiting for the opportune moment to sell me into slavery? You could be pretending to be one of the noble leaders of Clan Ardal, some broad-shouldered ruffian in disguise."

He growled at her, of the distinct impression she was having a laugh at him. Amusement flickered over her expression in fleeting hints of a smile. "You slept overnight in my lodge and ate my food. If I wanted to do some nefarious deed, such as selling you into slavery, the time's long passed."

"You're far too serious."

"She's hiding something. No one, let alone someone so

  Vivienne Savage

feeble and old, travels across not one but three kingdoms to retrieve a family heirloom. I don't believe she's told you the complete truth."

Victoria huffed and drew herself up, still coming barely past his shoulder. "I'm not a child, nor am I a fool. I'm certain you're right, she hasn't told us everything, but why should she? As you said, we're strangers. Still, I'm sure she isn't a threat."

"You're not leaving to help her, and that's final."

Victoria's eyes flashed with smoldering fury. "Final?" she sputtered. "You're not my bloody father."

"Technically, you placed me in charge of assisting you to the north."

"I didn't place you in charge of anything! You invited yourself along on *my* journey."

"And you'll be glad you have me along. What if she's a hag in disguise or some other dangerous creature here to prey on your naïveté?"

"A hag?" She snorted and crossed her arms. "Maybe you forget your own kingdom's history. Look what happened to Alistair for his unkindness. He was trapped as a dragon for years."

"That was a completely different situation!"

"How? What if she's a fairy and this is some test? Will you turn her away for no good reason?"

"What makes you—" The longer he considered it, the more plausible it became. With his brows raised, he glanced at the door and imagined Safiyya feigning sleep on the other side of it while plotting insidious tests. Victoria had "generously" volunteered his bed to the old woman, fearing she'd break her brittle bones on Talbot's or sink and disappear into Heldreth's mattress. "Your words have merit," he agreed grudgingly.

"Finally. Something sensible from you. Now if you don't mind, I would like to get some rest before we leave in the morning."

"Fine," he muttered.

When they returned inside and prepared for bed, Victoria changed behind the partition while he checked on the hearth fire. The storm may have blown over, but a damp chill remained in the air. He waited until he heard Victoria climb into bed before making his way over.

Ramsay piled blankets over Talbot's intolerable brick and stole a glance at Victoria. He didn't see much of her but golden hair, as if Heldreth's fluffy cloud had swallowed the rest of her whole.

The things he did to impress a woman. Why he wanted to impress her was what remained a mystery to him.

Chapter 4

Victoria awakened to the sight of darkened windows and the aroma of something unfamiliar and strong, exotic like spice. Ramsay lay on his back in his trousers on the adjacent bed, a shirtless mountain of a man who looked uncomfortable with several layers of blankets between him and the mattress.

The next empty bed had been made, and beyond the partition, she found Safiyya setting the table for three.

"Good morning to you, dear," the old woman said.

"Good morning, Safiyya. You cooked."

"Indeed, I have. It seemed the decent thing to do for one's benevolent hosts. Please. Have a seat."

As far as Victoria had seen, the older woman hadn't arrived with any supplies at all, yet she'd somehow prepared a breakfast without touching Ramsay's food stores. Perhaps they were dealing with a fae after all, and not a particularly clever one, to pull such an obvious trick out of thin air.

Pursing her lips, Victoria smiled and decided to play the game, feigning ignorance of her suspicions. "It was kind of you to go to the trouble."

"Please, have a seat and eat to your heart's content. Perhaps the big one will awaken and join us soon."

Victoria helped herself to one of the chairs. An array of unfamiliar fruit had been fanned over one of the wooden plates, its flesh pink and speckled with small seeds. She recognized sweet melon from Liang, a delicacy Anastasia's royal family had once imported to the castle, and tiny boiled eggs that couldn't have been laid by any chicken. The cup beside the breakfast held a dark substance like tar. She stared at it.

"Is something the matter?" Safiyya asked. Her violet eyes studied Victoria closely.

"Erm… It's so black," Victoria murmured, peering into the cup.

Safiyya's soft, musical laugh reminded Victoria of her cousin. "We call it coffee. Some find it to be a bitter drink, but it's prized for its invigorating traits." After a pause, the older woman added, "I find it most satisfying when mixed with cream and sugar."

Victoria fetched an adorable, bear-shaped honey crock from the counter then returned to the table. Ramsay still hadn't stirred. Following Safiyya's example, she added a large spoonful of honey to her mug and a small bit of cream before taking the first sip. She blinked in surprise.

"It's good."

"What's good?" Resembling a grumpy bear, Ramsay shuffled from behind the divider with sleep-mussed hair. His joints creaked for a few steps, and he groaned before rolling one shoulder.

"Pleasant night?" Victoria asked sweetly.

He grunted and dropped into the empty chair beside Victoria. Safiyya offered him a mug without cream.

"Here, I have a feeling you'll prefer it black," she said.

Ramsay gave the contents a single sniff then took a tentative swallow. His reluctance reminded Victoria of when she tried to convince her cousin's toddler to try new foods at the dinner table. After his first taste, he stared at the cup's dark contents again, then raised it to his mouth and chugged the remainder without stopping to breathe. Victoria giggled at his amazed expression.

"What did you call this?" he asked.

"Coffee," Safiyya replied. "It's quite popular in my homeland. When they roast the beans, the aroma travels on the wind for miles."

The old woman poured them each a second cup to enjoy with their breakfast. Victoria savored each bite of melon and mourned when the last pink cube disappeared from her plate. The eggs were delightful and buttery, golden inside without any white. Afterward, she cleaned up while Ramsay packed provisions for their journey.

"Would you like help?" Victoria asked him.

He grunted irritably. "I know what I want."

"Suit yourself," she replied, unable to fault him for grumpiness when he'd slept on a stone for her comfort.

Her father would have called her adventure a disaster and said it proved her survival skills to be insufficient, but a sense

of accomplishment pervaded her thoughts instead. Despite everything Duke Humphrey of Lorehaven had ever said to her, she had made friends and survived the exchange unmolested, without dishonor.

Smiling as she imagined the awe on her father's face when she arrived on her own without an armed escort, she stepped outside onto the sturdy porch to find Safiyya in the middle of the path. The woman wore her cloak again, long hair bound in a simple bun. Her hands were raised toward the sky, as if she were communing with nature.

Wary of interrupting her, Victoria skirted by the side of the cabin to tend to the horses. Rook and Ramsay's horse, Dunn, both stretched their heads over the chest-high gate to nose her in greeting. She stroked both and bided her time, brushing out her loyal steed.

Rook had the stamina and strength to bear two of them. Safiyya was a small slip of a thing, and Victoria weighed very little herself. "You're welcome to ride with me!" she called to the old woman.

"Completely unnecessary, my dear. I have a companion of my own."

The door opened and shut, and then Ramsay's heavy footfalls thudded down the steps before he came into view with enormous saddlebags and gear for the road.

Rook pressed his nose against Victoria's shoulder, inviting her to pet him. She stroked his neck and stole a quiet glance at Ramsay, to see him watching her in return. He chuckled and began outfitting his beast. No other horses stood beneath the lean-to.

Perhaps Safiyya wasn't some magical godmother and had arrived with an addled brain instead, an elderly grandmother with a family searching the hills after she'd walked off from their camp. "There are no other horses here, Safiyya."

The old woman's knowing smile said otherwise. She turned to the east and whistled. As the sharp note rose in volume and pitch, the wind stirred and kicked around fallen leaves. They spiraled in a rising column and came down to the ground again, swirling dirt and forest debris. When the dust settled, a glorious mare stood before them.

Victoria gasped and raised a hand to her mouth. Ramsay's brush hit the ground with a dull thump. All Safiyya did, however, was close the distance between them and place her palm against the ebony creature's coat. Her mane hung like liquid silver and moved despite the stillness of the air around them.

"I've never seen such a stunning creature in all my life," Victoria murmured. With uncanny intelligence in her electric blue eyes, the mare raised her proud head and nickered.

"Ruthaya is a dunestrider, a horse spirit of the desert wind, and she's traveled with me for many years. Or perhaps I should say, I've traveled with her. It's only by her generosity that I've made it this far from Samahara."

At a loss for words, Victoria struggled to contain her wonder, wanting to touch and stroke the mare but also wary of upsetting her. Shifters and fae were the most magical creatures she'd seen in all her life, and even those had become commonplace and typical for her over the years. Watching Alistair shift from a man to a dragon no longer terrified or intrigued her. He was simply a winged brother to her now.

"I see," Victoria murmured at last.

"I told you the old woman is hiding something," Ramsay whispered in her ear. "She's no fairy godmother, but she's hiding something from us. Yet you trust her. If she's a witch or a hag, I'll be the one to have to save you from the stewpot."

"You're an ass," Victoria whispered back.

"No, I'm a realist," he spoke without lowering his voice again. "Our guest arrived without any supplies, yet provided breakfast. She summoned an elemental with a whistle, a magical spell beyond mere parlor tricks."

"Ramsay, stop. You're behaving rudely. Are you always so high-strung and easy to worry?"

He made a disgruntled noise in his throat. "I am far from high-strung."

"You are."

"If I am, it's kept me alive a long time, lass. I've seen things in this world you couldn't imagine."

"You're not that old."

"Older than you," he snapped. "And wiser, too."

Safiyya cleared her throat. "I didn't mean to cause contention between you," the old woman said. "My apologies. I'll carry on alone without disrupting your travel plans."

"No," Victoria said firmly. "You don't have to do that, madam. There is no contention between us, because as far as I'm concerned, there is no *us* and Lord Ramsay is quite welcome to carry on alone."

"Victoria—"

"You are neither a king normy father," she seethed. "And I will not allow you to make my choices." She raised her chin, resolute in that decision. Triumph and terror battled for dominance, sending her heart into a frantic rhythm inside her chest.

Ramsay stared her down, equally as stubborn, but in the end, he looked away first and shrugged. "Then lead the way."

Chapter 5

With Ramsay and Dunn trailing behind them, Safiyya drew her mare beside Victoria and the two engaged in friendly small talk while ignoring the grumpy bear lagging to their rear. He may have been unhappy with the travel arrangements, but Victoria saw it as a learning opportunity, a chance to discover a world beyond Creag Morden and Cairn Ocland.

They traveled down a packed dirt road heading northward through Creag Morden, but if her memory of the kingdom's geography remained true, they'd cross a western path leading toward the Forest of the Ghost Winds—the vast woodland where her cousin had met with the fairy Eos years ago while fleeing for her life from a ruthless suitor.

"I haven't paid a visit to Lorehaven in years. It's different traveling on the ground. Before, Alistair flew Anastasia and me home on his back. I missed all of this."

"Ah, now I understand the marvel in your eyes as we travel," Safiyya remarked. "You have a beautiful country. The only meadows in Samahara are the ones bordering Liang and Ankirith, and even then, the rest of the kingdom is covered by the Ivory Sea and pockets of golden grass."

Victoria hadn't attended school as a child, instead educated by a strict governess who believed in teaching her etiquette above all else. She hadn't dabbled in geography and learning the rest of the world until a few years ago when Anastasia introduced her to Castle TalDrach's sprawling library. "The Ivory Sea is Samahara's largest desert, isn't it?"

"Yes. A desert so grand and so wide, men have died attempting to cross it."

"The stories I've read say your country is wondrous to behold. That you have crystals growing like flowers."

Safiyya's quiet laughter became a harsh, ragged cough she smothered in her robe sleeve. "Forgive me," she apologized once she'd taken a drink of water to clear her throat. "It is true, about the crystalline flowers. However, they only grow in one place. Samiran actually created the Jeweled Garden as a gift for me."

"Samiran?"

The joyous gleam in the old woman's eyes dimmed and she looked away. "Someone I lost long ago."

Ramsay's massive horse picked up speed, hooves thundering over packed dirt until he trotted beside the two women. "I think there may be trouble on the road. Look ahead," he said to them while pointing down the narrow highway. Farther ahead, a carriage lay on its side with a shattered wheel and no horses in sight.

"Bandits maybe?" Victoria asked.

"Most likely. We see them from time to time in Cairn

 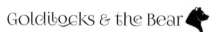

Ocland, venturing into our country to take advantage while we recover from our long battle with the Scourge. It's nothing new. Stay back and—"

Victoria urged Rook forward into a jog.

"Or you can do that," Ramsay muttered under his breath, words not lost to her even as she left him behind to investigate. She wouldn't be his simpering wallflower, not when she'd had such wonderful and fine examples of female Oclanders to emulate.

I can be as strong as them.

After slipping down from the saddle onto solid ground, she clutched Rook's reins in one hand and stepped up to the carriage. The door hung open on its hinges and the driver lay sprawled half beneath the toppled vehicle.

"He's dead," Victoria said. She rose from her crouch beside the corpse and looked around, uneasy. Goosebumps prickled against her skin, and she had the sense someone watched them.

"I told you there was trouble on the road," Ramsay muttered. He sniffed the air and his scowl deepened. "We should go before they return. Most likely, they'll be lurking nearby to await more travelers taking the northern pass."

"And leave them behind to harass and murder someone else?"

"It's no business of ours what they do on this road," Ramsay replied.

"Are you a coward or a bear?"

"Excuse me?"

Victoria raised her chin. "You heard me. I expected greater courage from a clan leader."

A deep growl rumbled in his chest, and for a moment, Victoria wondered if she had gone too far. Ramsay closed the distance between them and leaned into her, forcing her back a step.

"I am no coward."

An apology rested on the tip of her tongue until she remembered what Anastasia had told her about the bears. They were proud people, and they respected strength and backbone above all else. Instead of cowering or shrinking away, she stepped forward. "Then why run from danger?"

"My task is to escort *you*. Not purge your kingdom of bandits."

"Your self-appointed task?" she questioned him.

"If you think—"

"Please," Safiyya urged them in a strained voice. "There's no need for argument."

"There is," Victoria insisted.

"There's plenty of need when she wants to do a damned foolish thing."

"No," the old woman said. "There's no need, because your thieves are here."

The first bolt flew from the shadows of the forest bordering the highway. Ramsay shoved Victoria out of the way, knocking her to the ground.

"Stay down!" Ramsay roared at Victoria before adopting his larger form. Golden brown fur spread over his body, and then the cream tunic and green kilt blended away. Like most older shifters, he'd long ago mastered shifting between forms with his clothing intact between transformations.

Blood trickled out around the crossbow bolt lodged in his shoulder, a minor setback compared to the danger ahead of them. He charged with all his speed and became a caramel blur racing toward the treeline where their attackers had waited until the ambush.

I knew I smelled them nearby, Ramsay thought. Another bolt struck him, although it was as harmless as the first and landed in the meaty muscle of his upper arm.

Intimidated by the dire bear, his assailant cried out in a foreign tongue and turned to flee. Funny how a plea for help sounded the same in every language. The highwayman made it only a few steps before Ramsay slammed him into the hard earth. His black claws ripped leather armor and raked through skin. Blood welled beneath his heavy paw, and then he pulped the thief's torso with his weight.

Another robber materialized from the gloom of the forest as if he'd been invisible. Ramsay was certain he'd been looking at empty forest, an open space between two trees, moments ago. A narrow shaft of sunlight pierced the thick canopy, glinting off the bandit's blade as it came whistling toward

VIVIENNE SAVAGE

Ramsay's unprotected neck.

It never struck the target. Experience on the battlefield told the shifter what was happening before he saw it with his own eyes. The hairs on the back of his neck rose and the odor, like a coming storm, burned his sensitive nose.

Magic exploded from his left, creating a blinding flash and a deafening boom. The noise rang in Ramsay's ears, reminding him of the devastation caused by Queen Anastasia during the Battle of Mount Kinros when all the surviving clans rose against the oppressive black fae who'd cursed their lands.

The spell caught him unawares, and for a time, he thought it was an incantation meant for him until he reared back on both hind legs and realized he was unharmed. His vision slowly returned as he blinked away the after-image.

A man holding a pair of long swords with gleaming, curved edges lay alongside the road. Smoke rose from his chest and strange, branching lines had been seared into his skin. A glance toward Safiyya revealed the woman sitting astride her mount, watching him with her eerie violet eyes. They smoldered beneath her hood, twin plumes of purple flame.

I knew it. I knew there was something strange about her. She's no fairy godmother. She's a sorceress. After shrinking back to his human form, Ramsay ripped the bolt from his shoulder and tossed it aside. Sweet stars, it hurt. He pounded one fist against a tree trunk and growled while preparing himself to remove the second. Ripping it out of his bicep hurt more than the first, radiating the pain up and down his arm from the shoulder to the tips of his fingers.

"Victoria?" he called while wiping the blood from his hands.

The young woman had vanished. He spun to seek her but saw only verdant growth lining both sides of the road.

"Victoria!"

He found her on the opposite side of the road just beyond the edge of the treeline with blood smearing her fair hands, a dagger loosely held in one. Her owlish eyes stared back at him, and a dying man lay at her feet while choking on his final breaths. Bright scarlet arterial blood spurted from his open neck wound.

"He's dying," she said in a quiet, frail voice.

"Yes."

"I killed a man."

Ramsay gently pried the dagger loose from her trembling, red-smeared fingers and tucked it into his leather belt. "Yes. You did."

Before he could reach out and steady her, Victoria lurched away and vomited into a bush. He smoothed his hand up and down her back without saying a word. When she finished, he offered his canteen and a strip of rough linen torn from his shirt.

What the hell had the wolves taught her? She'd been by his side in the middle of the road one moment, and in seconds, she'd taken a roadside bandit by surprise.

"Safiyya," Victoria said when some of the color returned to her cheeks. She returned his canteen after another sip. "Where is she?"

He snorted. "Safe, last I saw. I believe she's well capable of defending herself after all. She's a sorceress."

Silence fell between them for a long while before she asked, "Is this where you say you told me so and rub it in my face that I was wrong?"

"No, lass." But someone else had once before, if not multiple times. Seeing the resignation in her eyes, he knew she'd become accustomed to such behavior. "But it is time we had a chat with our companion," he said as he tucked a strand of her hair behind one ear.

With the danger behind them, Ramsay guided Victoria from the brush and onto the road. To their great fortune, neither Rook nor Dunn had bolted during the scuffle, and both horses stood alongside Safiyya. She hadn't even taken them by the reins to keep them still.

"Are you well, dear?" Safiyya asked in a gentle voice.

"I… I believe so," Victoria replied.

Allowing his curiosity to get the better of him, Ramsay crouched beside the bandit and examined him. The rogue had been electrocuted on a clear, cloudless day, as if struck by a bolt of lightning. Although he found pearls and a woman's delicate coin purse, they weren't the valuables Ramsay wanted. He desired information.

He found that last when he turned over the thief's hand

and saw the number thirty-nine had been tattooed across the palm in an exaggerated style. Examination of the other bodies revealed similar tattoos, though with different numbers. Victoria had killed number forty and he had mauled thirty-seven.

"Who the hell numbers themselves like this?" he muttered.

"An infamous band from Liang," Safiyya answered. "I will tell you of them, but not here. We should go."

Returning his attention to Safiyya, the bear shifter searched her tired face. Her wrinkles had become more prominent, her face was weathered more than he recalled, and she slumped in her seat as if exhausted.

She'd certainly cast a spell, and he'd dare her to deny it, but first, getting the two women to safety had to be his priority. Still in shock from the trauma of taking her first life, Victoria stood listlessly beside him, silent.

"Are you able to ride?" he asked her.

"Yes."

"Then we should get away from here." If bandits one through thirty-seven were anywhere nearby, he didn't want to be present when they arrived. Ramsay shuddered. "If your map's correct at all, we ought to be coming to a village soon. It'll be a place for you to both rest."

"We will. Anastasia's maps are always correct."

He grunted and climbed astride Dunn.

By the time they concluded the first leg of their journey, the trees had finally thinned and a small village stretched before them. Stars twinkled in the distant sky as the sun set the horizon aflame in shades of citrine and rose.

"Not much of a welcome," Ramsay muttered as they rode into the small town. Distrustful villagers eyed them from afar without calling out greetings. Few people moved on the streets, and those who did quickly scuttled indoors.

Victoria pointed ahead of them to a two-level brick building, easily four times the size of the cottages they'd passed on the town's main road. "There's an inn. You can always tell from the chimneys." Three streams of smoke trailed into the air.

Ramsay dragged in a deep breath and filled his lungs with the aroma of roasting meat. His belly rumbled, and he realized how much he wanted a bite of something to eat besides bread and tough, dried venison.

They stabled Rook, Dunn, and Ruthaya next door. The nervous stableman barely made eye contact, and he cringed away from Ramsay when he tried to offer him money, as if expecting to be struck.

What's happening in this town? Ramsay wondered.

He opened the front door of the inn to reveal a quaint tavern not unlike the pubs of Cairn Ocland, the floor covered in hardwood planks and multiple round tables surrounded by hard-backed chairs. The strong smell of ale and stew drew him further inside.

"That smells delicious," Victoria said in a dreamy voice.

Studying them with wary eyes, the man behind the bar

tossed his washrag aside and straightened tall. One of his hands remained below the counter. "What do you need, strangers?"

He's holding a weapon out of sight. Expecting trouble, Ramsay thought as he removed a handful of coin. Silver traded well anywhere, even if it was Oclander money instead of the kingdom's currency. "A room for the night."

The barman relaxed. "Ah. Not to be ungrateful for your patronage, but Rosegate isn't a good place to be stopping right now."

"Why's that?" Ramsay asked.

"There are bandits on the road south of us, though they sometimes pay a visit to the local townsfolk. You may want to move on."

Safiyya's quiet chuckle sounded like a low croak, and Victoria eased into place beside Ramsay at the counter. He glanced at the two women then at the bartender. "Three bandits, right? One of them with a thirty-nine on his hand? We ran into those three on the south road."

"Ran into them?" the man questioned. His gaze dropped to the scarlet blood staining Ramsay's tunic.

"Aye. Ran into them. You'll be happy to know your trouble with the lot of them is done now."

Murmurs went up through the crowd gathered in the common room. The barkeep shushed them all and passed back the coins Ramsay had set on the counter.

"Upstairs, last door in the right hall. Your money is no good here."

"I can't—"

Victoria set her hand on his arm and shook her head. Relenting, he scooped up the coins. "Thank you."

The door opened into a large room with two beds. A wash basin sat behind a carved divider and a neat stack of wood rested beside a small hearth on the far wall. While not opulent, it looked cozy and clean. More importantly, it *smelled* clean. Victoria drew in a deep breath and released it on a content exhalation.

"What are you doing?" Ramsay asked.

"Enjoying a proper room."

"Was my cabin not 'proper' enough?"

A quick rush of heat surged into her face, followed by a cold knot in her stomach. "No, that's not what I meant."

When Ramsay swept past her into the room, she regretted her poor choice in words. Ever the sensible source of comfort, Safiyya patted her arm then followed the bear inside. The old woman moved directly to a chair and sank down onto the cushioned seat.

"A whole town terrified by three bandits?" Victoria said as she closed the door behind them. "That doesn't make much sense."

"The typical traveler isn't prepared for an ambush along the road, and this town has no guards from what I've seen," Ramsay said. "In Cairn Ocland, most villages have a personal militia and people willing to fight for what's theirs. I saw nothing here but scared people."

Victoria frowned. Throughout her childhood and adult life in Creag Morden, she only recalled the king's personal guard in the city and her royal entourage whenever she traveled across the kingdom with her family or to society functions among the nobility. They weren't like the neighboring kingdom of Dalborough, wealthy enough to post men in every tower.

Suddenly cold, Victoria wrapped her arms around herself and drifted to the narrow window. "We've never needed guards all over the kingdom. We've never had bandits either."

"Which makes for easy pickings and tells me one thing," Ramsay muttered. He crossed his arms against his chest and studied both women. "Those highwaymen weren't expecting a shifter *or* a sorceress."

"No, I daresay they were not," Safiyya agreed. "Of course, I hadn't expected a shifter either. I assumed you were of this kingdom, Ramsay."

He grunted in response and moved over to the hearth. "Victoria knows exactly who I am. What we don't know is who you really are. If we're going to harbor you and help you to the north, I think we deserve to know what in the stars happened out there. I know magic when I see it, and you're far from being some helpless old crone."

"I never claimed to be helpless," Safiyya said.

Victoria stared at the old woman, mouth agape. "Then you *are* a fairy godmother."

"I am no fairy, child. I am Safiyya, Enchantress of Ankirith's Opal Spire."

Ramsay stared without any acknowledgment of the woman's claim, his brows drawn together in a familiar look of confusion, but recognition struck Victoria at once.

"You can't be Enchantress Safiyya," she blurted out. "There's no way she'd be alive today. I've read stories about her written centuries ago. In fact, I've read those same stories to my cousin's daughter so many times I… It simply isn't possible."

"Yet it is so."

Ramsay frowned. "But that would make you…"

The woman leveled her violet gaze at them. "Incredibly old, young man. I have seen the rise and fall of several empires and kingdoms since my birth. But my magic is waning. Soon, there will be nothing left of it, and I find myself in a predicament."

"You need our help," Victoria breathed. "All this time, I was certain we had encountered a fairy godmother sent to test us."

Safiyya's shoulders fell, proud posture diminishing more with each second. Her fragile smile vanished. "If only it could be so simple and easy. I find myself at your mercy. Those stories are nothing more than tales of a time long past, and what you see before you now is all that remains of the once-great Enchantress Safiyya."

Victoria shot Ramsay a dirty look when he snorted then returned her attention to Safiyya. No. She refused to allow such an accomplished woman to pity herself now. "Then what may we do to help you, Enchantress? As you've spent all your life at the service of others, it's only fair for you to receive help when you need it most."

"You are a kind girl, Victoria. Thank you." Safiyya released a pent-up breath. When she continued, her voice wavered with emotion. "I didn't lie, exactly, when I said Aladdin stole something of great value to me. What I neglected to share was that the item had been in the possession of another wizard at the time of its theft."

"And what was this item of great value?" Victoria asked.

"He stole a lamp."

"He stole a lamp," Ramsay repeated.

"It is the prison of my husband, Samiran, an ifrit from the Ivory Sea."

"Excuse me," Victoria said. "I believe I misheard you. An ifrit? I don't understand what that means."

"It is a word without direct translation in your language. They are what your people might call a…" Safiyya appeared to search for a word, quieting before she gazed at them with her unusual violet eyes. "Not a fairy, but a powerful spirit of fire."

"An elemental, like your horse," Ramsay said.

"Close enough, yes. Many years ago, before you were even born, or your great-grandmother was born, Samiran was captured by a foul sorcerer and placed in this special lamp—a lamp of binding, a tool used to subjugate the ifrit and their lesser jinn cousins who are tricked, or worse, have broken their word to a mortal."

"And you've waited all of this time to mount a rescue?" Ramsay demanded.

"No, young bear," Safiyya murmured. "A year ago, I unveiled the location of Samiran's captor, but arrived much too late to liberate him. The wizard had been slain and his vaults emptied by a famed assassin."

Ramsay's tensed posture relaxed. "So now you follow this assassin?"

"Yes. After much searching, I discovered it was Aladdin and his men who had ransacked the wizard's treasures. But from there, his trail vanished." Appearing smaller and frailer by the moment, Safiyya dipped her head. "I failed Samiran."

I didn't think such dedication existed in all of the kingdoms, Victoria thought. "You must truly love him to spend so many years seeking his freedom."

"Not as long as I wish. For centuries, I thought he had abandoned us and I allowed our son to become a bitter adult believing the same thing. And then the truth came to me from a traveling alchemist from Liang." Safiyya dabbed her eyes with the edge of her robes. "So I ask you, no, plead with you to please help me. I want to see him again. One last time before there's nothing left of me. More than anything, I want him to be free."

This was it. A chance to help someone in need while making her own unique mark on the world. Nervous excitement buzzed through Victoria, raising the hairs on her arms when she thought of going up against a famed thief. Although he'd told her only in the strictest confidence, Griogair had been one in his youth—long, long ago before he found his way as a law-abiding citizen—and he'd taught her many tricks of the trade he no longer practiced. Going unseen and moving in silence were only a few among the talents she'd learned.

"I'll help," Victoria said. She glanced up to her left at Ramsay. While she expected judgment and even condemnation on the unyielding bear's face, she saw moisture in the corners of his eyes and compassion instead. At last, *something* had moved him.

"Aye. Help you shall get then. Tell us what we need to know and how it's to be done, Safiyya."

"I'll begin with what I've learned since I began my journey. The gang of bandits once belonged to Aladdin's brother, a ruthless man named Ali Baba."

Victoria leaned forward. "But then?"

"Aladdin murdered his own kin in cold blood and assumed his place." Safiyya turned to Ramsay. "You noticed the strange number tattoos, did you not? That is how they mark themselves. He has forty in all, each deadlier than the last."

"Thirty-seven now," Ramsay muttered.

"How did they make their way beyond Cairn Ocland without being captured?" Victoria asked. "King Alistair is my cousin's husband, and their shifters patrol the countryside in force, hunting for opportunistic brigands and poachers from Liang."

"Better yet, how did they acquire a lamp from a wizard? Aren't the Liangese among the most powerful in all the lands?"

"They are, but even a wizard has his weaknesses. How they overcame him was not my concern. What troubles me is that my Samiran wasn't there when I arrived. The only logical explanation was they forced him to grant a wish. Transporting a gang of over forty men would be a small feat for one as powerful as Samiran. So I searched. My discovery of their whereabouts in this kingdom was the result of many weeks of scrying."

"Then you began your travels."

"I had already arrived in Liang hoping to free Samiran, so I simply continued my journey northward. Even with Ruthaya as my companion, it took many months to cross their vast empire. Cairn Ocland was a rather pleasant interlude in comparison."

Ramsay snorted. "You must have arrived after we cleansed the Scourge."

Safiyya tilted her head to one side. "I sensed a dissipating darkness, yes. Your Scourge?"

"A long story for another time," Ramsay said. "For now, what's your plan? Forgive me, but even with your impressive display against the bandits, you don't seem capable of performing such an act of sorcery again. You need rest."

"My plan is a simple one. While scrying for signs of Samiran, I discovered a few other magical items. Items that I can use. Items in *this* kingdom."

"The only magical items we have in Creag Morden are wands," Victoria said. "Is that what you need?"

"No, what I need is much stronger. I had thought to convince you to part ways with me at the first town we reached so I could go after it, but our furry friend is correct. I do lack the power to carry on without aid."

Overwhelmed with sympathy, Victoria tried to imagine the enchantress going off alone on a quest for love and knew she'd never forgive herself if she didn't accompany her. If Safiyya could travel across kingdoms, an old woman with dwindling magical reserves, then surely Victoria could help her on the way.

Griogair would be proud of her for putting his lessons to good use.

"What is it that you need, Safiyya?" Victoria asked, confident in her decision. "I'll do whatever is within my power to help you."

"A hammer. The hammer of a jewelsmith held in great honor, for he was the master artisan behind the invention of many great discoveries. It is only with this hammer that the gnomes were able to make and unmake enchanted items."

Understanding dawned upon Victoria at once. "You want to use it to free Samiran."

"Yes. It was once in my ability as a sorceress to do this without such a tool, but I've grown old and used much of my power to extend my life."

"And is that it?"

Little by little, the light and confidence returned to Safiyya's eyes. "There's one more thing…"

The shifter's golden brows raised. "What is it?"

"While the hammer is most important, there's also a ring I hope you'll find while exploring. I can't retrieve it with my own hands. It must be given to me."

"And why's that?" Ramsay asked without any condescension in his voice. Genuine curiosity deepened a crease across his forehead.

"Because the jinni bound to the ring I require is an ancestor of mine."

Chapter 6

AFTER A LONG day of riding, nothing could have felt better to Ramsay than sleeping on a comfortable bed. While the mattress in the inn wasn't to his preference, it beat Heldreth's veritable cloud and Talbot's sheet of iron. He awakened without an aching back and that was all that mattered.

He didn't know what to make of their current situation. Ifrit, jinn, and enchantresses were well beyond his understanding. Even the fae common to his homeland were a nuisance, better avoided at all costs. Victoria's romantic notions about godmothers had never made sense to Ramsay, having seen firsthand the havoc they caused by meddling in the affairs of humans and shifters alike. In fact, he had been grateful none of the troublemakers had taken an interest in Clan Ardal's children.

While both women slept in their shared bed, he made his way downstairs into the quiet common room and requested breakfast. Since they hadn't let him pay for the room, he left a hefty tip before taking a tray of sausage, griddle cakes, and porridge upstairs. The low murmur of feminine voices carried through the doorway.

"Are you decent?" he called out.

Victoria answered by opening the door, fully dressed. Her cheerful gaze fell on the tray first then rose to his face.

"I swear you're a mind reader. We were just discussing breakfast."

They had been discussing more than food, he figured, spotting Safiyya with the map spread out across the bed. While he divided portions of sweet cakes and savory sausage, the two women sat together and planned their excursion.

"How far is this hammer you need?" Victoria asked.

Safiyya drew her crooked finger over the artfully depicted terrain. "Here."

"But there's nothing there," Victoria exclaimed. "It's a ravine."

"You only know what's on the surface, my dear. There is much more beneath. An entire city, in fact."

"What? No, that's impossible. Unless…" Victoria hesitated and bit her lower lip.

"Unless what?" Ramsay asked. He disliked the ashy pallor that had come into her cheeks.

Victoria fidgeted, shifting one leg over the other. "There's an old legend, a bedtime story really, about an ancient king who ruled with an iron fist. His people dwelled underground and were said to come up to the surface at night to steal away children. But our mothers and fathers always told us they would only steal away naughty children."

"The Gnome King," Safiyya confirmed. "And it is no

 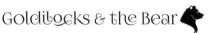

legend. Some of it has been exaggerated over the years, I'm sure, but a greed like his doesn't occur without consequences."

Victoria leaned forward. "What consequences?"

"They say your ancestors put an end to him, but it's there that the story becomes murky at best. Something was done. The citizens of Creag Morden grew tired of nightly raids by the gnomes. They would breach the surface like a plague of locusts to steal whatever children they could to work their deep mines."

"So they did kidnap children?"

"Yes. By the hundreds. You see, gnomes were a crafty bunch, and they gladly devoted their time toward developing machinery and gearcraft. But what time does such a thing leave for mines and manual labor?"

The bitter taste of nausea rose in Ramsay's throat. "Why children?"

"Easier to control. Easier to break. A grown man can overpower an unarmed gnome, but the same isn't true for a child. Plus, children fit better into narrow shafts and have little hands capable of prying small stones from crevices."

"That's awful," Victoria breathed.

"It was quite awful, though it was a time long before I was born. Before I became the enchantress of the Opal Spire, my mother served as its lorekeeper. Unfortunately, I found the tale in an incomplete tome, and I know not how your ancestors overcame their enemy. What I do know is that the gnomes are long gone."

"So you're saying, somehow, a ring holding an ancestor of yours ended up in a gnomish city." Ramsay peered closer at the map and frowned.

Safiyya nodded. "Yes, a ring crafted by the most talented of the city's jewelsmiths and bound by magic. Then, it was in high fashion for members of noble families across the continent to own a ring bound by the spirit of a jinni. Over time, these trinkets were lost, and like many other things in history, no one else remembers."

Like Maeval the Black Fae, Ramsay thought, wondering what other secrets the world had forgotten.

"The gorge isn't far from here. A day's ride at most," Victoria said. "We could set out right now."

"Perhaps another day of rest is in order," Ramsay suggested. Contrary to Victoria's eagerness, Safiyya's haggard appearance didn't convince him she'd survive a stiff wind.

"No," Safiyya murmured. "Time is crucial to our success."

Despite his gut inclination to allow Safiyya time to recuperate from their rough journey, they set out within the hour and continued a northwestern journey. Once the sun began to descend, Ramsay insisted on stopping for the night. The expected protests never came. They made camp then resumed with the sunrise.

By midafternoon, they reached the gorge. Grass grew in verdant pockets amidst the rocks and a noisy waterfall crashed in the distance, dispersing a cool mist into the air. Ramsay reached out and dragged his fingers across the indigo-tinged stone.

"Ana and I became lost here once, many years ago," Victoria said as they navigated the treacherous, rocky slopes. Bits of loose rock crumbled beneath their horses' hooves. "We wandered away from the royal entourage."

"I have a hard time believing you were a disobedient child," Ramsay said.

"Admittedly, it was Ana's idea. She was always the bolder of us, but I followed along anyway."

Victoria spoke so little about her childhood as a noble's daughter that he found himself curious. "What happened?"

"It was fun at first. We chased each other through the twisting paths. But then a rainstorm came. I remember how the thunder echoed off the rock walls, sounding like an explosion. My pony threw me, and Ana's mare injured herself on the rocks. We ended up walking for what seemed like forever in the rain before the guards found us."

Safiyya chuckled beside them.

A grin slipped onto Ramsay's face too. "Did you get in trouble?"

"No, but we both spent days in bed together coughing and sneezing." She gazed at the path ahead of them with a wistful smile on her face. "Both of our fathers said that was punishment enough since it meant we didn't get to enjoy the days spent at the summer retreat. Still, I don't remember any caverns or city entrances."

"Ah, but you weren't looking for them either," Safiyya said.

Victoria's smile widened. "Certainly not, but if Anastasia had known, she would have dragged me along for the search."

Traversing another mile of uneven terrain led them to a mossy wall beside a cavernous opening. Directly right, water spilled down the mountainside and formed a pool beside them. Forced to dismount, they left the horses to drink and stepped inside.

"This way." Safiyya summoned a small flame between her hands. It started as a mere spark then grew to the size of an apple while hovering above her palms. The flickering light revealed an ordinary narrow crevice, barely more than an alcove.

He began to wonder if Safiyya had reached the age of senility. "*This* is the gnome city?"

She laughed at him. "Of course not." She reached into the alcove, and then her hand passed through the rock face. "This is but the pathway to reach the city. You two must travel deep into the heart of the cave before you find the doors. The path will be marked."

While Victoria clapped her hands together in amazement, Ramsay blinked and waved his hand through the illusionary wall too. "I stand corrected."

"We'll return with your ring and the hammer," Victoria vowed while taking Safiyya by the hands. "But will you be all right here?"

"Although I've attempted to conserve enough of my power, Ruthaya will come to my aid if necessary. Now that we've arrived, I wonder how I ever thought I could explore this city on my own." Her fragile smile diminished. "Take care of yourselves, and one warning before you go. Whatever you do, no matter how dire the situation seems, don't summon the jinni in the ring. He'll try to trick you, as is their nature."

Victoria unfastened her light crossbow and handed it to the old woman. "It would make me feel better if you kept this at hand."

"I have magic, love."

"And if it should fail you, as magic sometimes does, this will be here. Let's hope you need nothing more."

Ramsay removed a small lantern from his pack then slung the heavy bag's strap crosswise over his brawny shoulders. The brown leather bag settled just above his hip. "Do me the honor, Safiyya?"

With one frail hand, the sorceress touched the tip of the wick and created a blue flame. "This should last you for a while."

"Thank you. Take care and be safe until we return." With his other hand, he took Victoria by the shoulder and guided her toward the path.

Cool air greeted them inside the cavern, and the dank smell of wet stone and moss accompanied the sound of dripping water. The first thirty yards took them around a subtle leftward curve on a descending slope.

"Are you certain you wouldn't prefer to remain outside with Safiyya?" Ramsay asked.

"I'm certain. As much as I'd like to keep her safe, I'd be of better use in here with you." Her gaze roved over his broad chest. "We're heading into a cave after all, and there may be places where you won't fit. I may not be as tiny as a gnome, but I'm smaller than you."

Following Safiyya's directions, Ramsay and Victoria stuck to a narrow track marked with runes carved into the stalagmites. They traveled through an open archway into a narrow corridor. The candle flickered, the cobalt light dimming for no apparent reason, leaving Ramsay to rely on his shifter eyesight to see.

"That's strange, isn't it?" Victoria asked.

"It's discomforting, yes." Ramsay looked down at the tiny flame and frowned. He sensed a heaviness in the air, a disquieting aura that made him want to turn back and drag Victoria away from the wretched place.

"Look, the walls have a slight glow to them. I wonder if—" Squealing, she lurched forward and stumbled.

Ramsay reached out and caught her by the arm before his eyes dropped to see what had tripped her. The skeleton of a man, or maybe even a female adventurer, lay in dried and brittle leathers. The murderer must have bludgeoned them, because he noticed a huge hole in the skull. An untouched pack remained beside it.

It took only a few moments to locate more skeletal remains. The bodies had been scattered without rhyme or reason, many of them left out in the open near the exit of the rectangular chamber.

"Do you suppose wild animals may have come and broken them this way?" Victoria asked.

"No. I doubt it. You see this?" he asked her while nudging a skeleton with the toe of his boot. "All the pieces are present. They're merely shattered. An animal would carry the parts it desires and be away from this place. This… this is something else."

"What do you think killed them?"

He shrugged. "Could be anything, but whatever it is, it's long gone, I think. These bones are ancient."

The faint light gleamed on something ahead. A few steps closer revealed a door crafted from dull metal. Unrecognizable runic words had been carved across the top.

"Do you understand a word of that?" he asked her.

"Not one," Victoria replied while tracing her fingertips over the letters.

"I'd say we found the front door," Ramsay mused. "Not very fancy, is it? I'd expected something a little grander."

"There's a keyhole, but Safiyya didn't give us a key."

Dismayed, he glanced toward the path behind them. "We'll have to find another way into this supposed gnomish city then, won't we?"

Before he could suggest an alternative, Victoria opened one of the leather pouches on her belt and removed a pickset. She crouched in front of the keyhole with an expression of tremendous concentration on her face.

Like all other bears of Clan Ardal, Ramsay had inherited the ability to stonecraft with mere thought. Thinking to help her, he reached out into the earth around them and found only a barren, empty force.

What in the name of the stars?

Somehow, the gnomes had completely cut him off from his gift. Glancing left and right, he squinted at the markings etched into the walls and frowned. Magical runes against interference glowed pale green, emitting a luminescent light. That must have been it.

Tumblers clicked and whirred while machinery made noisy and ominous sounds above them.

"Victoria—"

"Just a minute now. I've almost got it."

An unseen mechanism clanked and whirred as an installation in the wall responded to her actions.

"Victoria, something is happening," Ramsay warned again. The hairs on his nape rose and cold sweat beaded on his brow. "You must have set off some kind of trap, lass."

"Then stop distracting me," she hissed back at him over a shoulder.

Dust and bits of crumbling debris fell around them like snow, and the grinding continued while Ramsay searched above them. The ceiling had begun to move, lowering on a smooth track.

Sharpened stalactites jutted toward them in quantities too numerous to count. One had a skull stuck to it. Suddenly, the skeletal remains made sense. Thieves and grave robbers had been speared and crushed for their attempts to rob the city.

"Hurry!"

The tumblers clicked and the door rolled into the ground, opening a passage into the next room. Above them, the ceiling came down faster and showered them with bits of rock and grit. Ramsay lunged forward. Before Victoria had the chance to rise from the ground, he collided with her and the force carried them both over the threshold.

A thunderous crash roared behind them as the ceiling came down.

Victoria remained quiet and still beneath him, her breaths coming as quick as a frightened bird's. But she didn't argue or voice a single complaint. His chest heaved with panic while his brain attempted to reconcile the reality of how close they had come to death.

Seconds. Mere seconds.

"We're not dead," she finally whispered in a strained, hoarse voice.

"No, not yet. Are you hurt?"

"I can't breathe," she wheezed.

"What? Why? What hurts, Victoria?" he asked in a worried rush.

"You're squishing me."

After rising onto his elbows, Ramsay blinked down at her. Their tumble into the next corridor had placed him square above Victoria while her body twisted beneath him, partially on her side. With unyielding stone beneath her and his broad-shouldered physique crushing her into the ground, it was no wonder she couldn't breathe.

"Sorry," Ramsay muttered. After he climbed off and helped Victoria to her feet, she rolled her left wrist. He took it between both of his hands and caressed the fragile joint with his thumb.

"A little sore but nothing seems broken." Her blue gaze rose to make eye contact, pale face highlighted by the glowing runes on the walls. "Thank you."

"Don't worry about it. We've got bigger problems now, lass. The way out is sealed shut, and we'll be down here for the unforeseeable future if there isn't another exit."

"Can't you use your magic to clear it?"

"No. It seems I can't. I tried while you were picking the lock, and it's like trying to grip a wet fish. There are disruptive runes everywhere. Leads me to think the wee buggers designed this to keep my ancestor kin out."

"It's probable. What would be the point of going to such extraordinary effort, only for someone to carve their way inside your home with magic? It's no wonder others have died before us."

Victoria shivered. He set an arm around her shoulders and wondered if she'd begun to regret her fantastic adventure yet. If it wasn't living up to the romantic expectations she'd had when she'd set out from Castle TalDrach.

At first, she stiffened beneath his arm, but then she relaxed into his side. "We'll find a way out. According to lore and old

 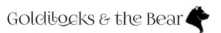

tales, the gnomes were ingenious little buggers. I'd expect them to be too wise to have only a single entrance to the city. There'll be another way out."

"Then let's find it."

They set out at once down the widening corridor into a reception hall lined by statues. There they discovered the skeletal remains of two fallen guardsmen, their little bodies still adorned by armor. A shattered lantern lay beside them, its alchemical innards strewn beside the metal framework and shards of glass. It no longer glowed.

"I wonder if there was an attack," Ramsay mused as they stepped over them through the open city gate.

Victoria glanced sadly back at the gnomish guardsmen. "Perhaps there was. They certainly weren't killed by a falling ceiling."

"Look over here," Ramsay said, calling her attention to the fountain in the center of the room. Water continued to bubble out of the decorative fixture. "This has all been carved from gemstone. I've never seen anything like it, not at this scale."

"What do you mean?"

"It's been shaped from a single gem, Victoria. Have you ever seen one so large? I could do this and make a small figurine."

"So they had the same powers as Clan Ardal?"

"Could be. That or they were craftsmen beyond compare."

With little else to see beyond the beauty of the gnomish statuary, they continued forward down a flight of stairs onto an expansive terrace with calf-high walls serving as a rail. Down below, a dizzying view revealed a world larger than Cairn Ocland's largest city. Although it appeared to be a ghost city without a single moving soul, hundreds, if not thousands of lights gleamed from behind city windows stacked multiple stories high.

Ramsay backed away from the edge and closed his eyes.

"Are you… are you afraid of heights?" Victoria asked.

"Of course not," he snapped. He drew in a deep breath through his nose then cracked his eyes open to look again. The sickening sense of nausea tightened his stomach.

It was as terrifying the second time as it had been the first. Bears weren't meant to be so high off the ground.

"You *are*," Victoria breathed. "It makes you feel absolutely sick, doesn't it? Being a thousand feet above ground, able to plummet to the bottom at any—"

"Stop!" he roared at her, close to the point of dry retching. Even though he'd closed his eyes, the entire world continued to spin, as if the sight had been burned into his vision.

Victoria quieted. "I'm sorry. That was childish and cruel of me. Here." Her small hands and cool fingers touched his bare arm. "Come with me. I'll lead you to the stairs."

"We're underground," he grumbled. "We shouldn't be thousands of feet above the floor."

He trusted her, although it seemed they walked for miles.

"Don't look yet. I think I've found something."

The soles of his boots struck hard metal instead of stone.

 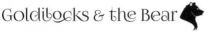

The thuds of his footfalls echoed gently, and then Victoria led him forward. While the ground remained stable and firm beneath him, the sense of swaying rhythm made him open his eyes.

He discovered a metal frame around them, although the front opened to reveal the terrace. Another skeleton lay in the corner on the solid metal floor, and what he assumed were gnomish numbers glowed in pale blue runes on the wall beside a huge lever.

"This reminds me of the dumbwaiter in the castle," Victoria murmured. She pulled on the lever.

"What are you doing? We shouldn't mess with this."

"Why not?"

Before he could cross the box to stop her, she threw her weight into the switch. The door swung shut with a creaking groan. Then the box dropped.

Sparks rained down around them as something squealed above the ceiling. Metal scraped against metal while Ramsay screamed throughout most of the fall. Each second of his thirty-eight years passed before his eyes in terrifying detail until at last the motion stopped and they hung still.

"We've reached the first floor. What a nice contraption!"

Ramsay stared at her long after she threw open the gate and stepped outside. He followed her onto solid, beautiful ground and suppressed the urge to kiss it and promise to never leave it again. "How did you know it would work?"

"I didn't."

"We could have plummeted to our deaths!"

"It would have been ten seconds of the most exciting ride of our lives then," Victoria replied. "This is amazing. Truly. I can see the track and the cables."

When he glanced above them, he saw an immeasurable length of metal extending toward the sky, resembling a vertical variant of the goblin mine carts. *Were* the goblins distant relatives of the gnomes? Focusing on that mystery allowed him a brief reprieve from the terror she'd inflicted on him.

"You would have suffered more and far longer had I led you down the stairs by the hand," Victoria said defensively. She reached for his hand and took it between both of hers before caressing his knuckles like she was comforting a small child. "The worst is over now."

"Fine." Her touch soothed him and took the edge off his anger, calming the rush of his pulse thumping inside his head. Resigned to forgive her, he scrubbed a hand down his face. "On the way back, though, I think I'll stick to the stairs. I'll find a way to tolerate it." And survive the vertigo.

As they strode forward together into the city, Ramsay remained keenly aware that Victoria hadn't released his hand yet. From the lift, the paths diverged into three distinct paths lit by glowing streetlamps, and the trails wound out of sight into what he presumed were different districts of the city. To their direct right, stairs led on a winding path toward the upper terrace.

"I didn't expect the place to be so large," Victoria admitted while glancing at the sign post written in indecipherable gnomish. "How are we supposed to find a ring in all of this?"

"You didn't expect it to be easy, did you?"

"Well, no." Disappointment tugged the corners of her mouth into a deep frown. "I don't know what I expected, but I certainly don't see a castle, do you?" She huffed, the sharp breath stirring her bangs.

"No, but the goblins don't have castles either. Still, their leaders have markedly different homes. The commoners all dwell within niches carved into the walls, similar to how a bee stores its honey. Goblins only use their homes for sleeping, so there's room for nothing else inside them."

"Only sleeping?" she questioned.

"Aye. They don't read, study, or do quiltwork, lass."

"But what about…?"

As her voice trailed, he heard the subtle laughter. As he cut his gaze to the left, Ramsay caught a shy smile on her face.

Miss Prissy Daughter of a Noble had joked about sex? Taken by surprise and bewildered by her suggestive question, he almost missed his opportunity to taunt her in return. "Are you truly wanting to know what goes on between goblins?"

"Know what? I was only asking where they do their cooking," she said innocently. "You should get your mind out of the gutter, Ramsay. It's impolite." Without looking back, she flounced ahead of him.

"Brat," he muttered under his breath.

"It was a serious question," she insisted, despite her warm

laughter. "I've never seen a goblin city. When did you visit them?"

"After the battle against Maeval, I accompanied the goblins back to their home. It wasn't anything so grand as this." Ramsay gestured to the lovingly carved buildings around them. "More like holes cut into the walls, but the leader had a larger hollow with decorations and such outside."

"I'd heard of goblins while I lived in Creag Morden, but I always thought them to be little more than savage monsters under the mountains. Princess Teagan taught us otherwise."

"They're smart, aye. And the only thing savage about the wee buggers is their ability to fight. They may be small, but they're mighty given a sword. Or shard of metal. Or anything remotely resembling a weapon." Ramsay chuckled and let the tension ease from his spine, though his amusement soon faded.

No matter where he and Victoria searched, they encountered only skeletons and the remains of people long dead for centuries, nearby evidence implying they'd died during everyday activities.

"What happened here?" he wondered.

"I don't know. The city is as beautiful now as I suspect it was then. It's as if everyone simply… stopped living all at once. An illness? Magic?"

"A mystery for another time, lass."

What he presumed to be a lantern rested on the edge of a rail. Several dull spheres hung suspended in viscous liquid, and when he shook it, it surged with yellow light. Ramsay ventured forward with the lantern in one hand. Its golden glow cast shadows over the pillars to his left and right when he twisted to take in their surroundings.

"I suggest we head for the center of the city. That's where we'll likely find the gnome king's residence and, hopefully, the ring."

"Well, you have the light, so lead the way."

Venturing forward brought them winding through a city district occupied by low counters and shop stalls. Glass-paned storefronts between narrow corridors revealed jewelry, clocks, and trinkets. Victoria ducked inside a shop through a tiny door no taller than her hip and was forced to crouch while inside to navigate the cramped space.

Ramsay unclenched his fist when she emerged covered in dust. "Nothing?"

"Nothing."

They continued onward, pausing once to share water and a light snack. Another hour passed without any seeming progress through the strange city.

"This is worse than the maze garden at the castle," Victoria muttered. "Didn't we pass this building before?"

Ramsay glared at their surroundings. Every structure looked the same as the last and every door became identical. "All right, we've wandered in circles long enough. I suggest finding a place to hunker down for the night—morning, whatever damned time of day it is beyond these walls—and rest. It'll all make sense once we've had sleep."

"There was that small home back down the last corridor. The one we stuck our heads in, remember?"

"Lead the way then. I'm lost. We bears may enjoy caves, but we were never meant to be this far belowground."

Victoria wound her way back to the home with confidence, but then her steps faltered and she hesitated two steps beyond the threshold. "There are bodies here as well."

"There are bodies everywhere."

"Could we… remove them first? I can't sleep where there are corpses."

An argument waited on the tip of his tongue until he recalled her kindhearted gesture on the terrace when she'd attempted to shield him from facing the stairs. "I'll do it," he said gruffly.

While Victoria explored the small home, he hauled the remains of a family outside. Inside, they found beds far too small for their human-sized bodies. Each bunk had been carved into the walls, resembling the open crypt of a mausoleum with a thin mattress and blankets.

"They're sort of lumpy."

"That's because they're not filled with feathers. Moss or lichen, judging by the smell. It's everywhere outside." Ramsay shrugged and dragged one out. "If you grab the one from the other room we can lay them out on the floor."

After retrieving enough mattresses from the adjacent homes, they beat them thoroughly outside with a broomstick then spread them side by side and nose to end to create a large pallet on the floor.

"Do you think Safiyya will be all right?" Victoria asked as she sat cross-legged on her side of the makeshift bed.

Ramsay shrugged out of his cloak and set it aside. His bones protested the long day of travel compounded with hours of crawling in and out of buildings meant for tiny men and women. "I'm sure she will." At the girl's continued worried expression, he added, "She's got Rook, Dunn, and Ruthaya with her, lass, in addition to shelter in the cavern."

"I know. I just didn't expect to be here so long."

"Adventures are rarely quick and easy."

Victoria's gaze drifted to the equipment Ramsay had set to the side. "I'm sorry for teasing you about packing for a battle," she said.

He chuckled and passed her another blanket. "There's nothing to forgive. Are you cold?"

"A little. There has to be a way to warm these homes."

During their exploration, he hadn't seen anything resembling a fireplace. "Whatever marvel the gnomes used is lost to us. We'll have to settle for the blankets."

To Victoria's amusement, the gnomish blanket barely covered his shins and thighs, leaving his feet exposed. She laughed at him. With the leftover blankets, she piled three over her lower body and laid her head against his shoulder.

Victoria's hair no longer smelled like fresh flower petals, but he drew her closer against him just the same.

"Ramsay…?"

"What?" he asked innocently. "Would you like to be warmer or not?"

"It's not…"

"Not what?"

A few seconds of silence passed, her quiet breaths in the still air the only sound before she whispered, "Proper."

"What isn't proper about it?"

He didn't expect her to answer at all that time, her silence as telling as the rumors he'd heard of their strange, backward nation where physical pleasure was discouraged and held in disdain. Where bonds were only recognized after expensive and public rituals.

"An unwed woman isn't supposed to lay down with a man. It's inappropriate."

"Why?" Ramsay asked, reminding her of Anastasia's youngest child.

"I…"

"It's only sleeping beside one another."

The shifter didn't remove his arm. She hated and loved him for it, because he radiated more than enough warmth to make up for the insufficient heating, the lack of proper blankets, and the paper-thin mattresses that must have felt like feather beds to the gnomes. While she wanted to burrow into him and relish every second, the part of her born and raised a lady screamed at her to resist and pull away.

Resisting Ramsay shouldn't have been so hard, especially

when he'd made no sexual offers or advances. All he had done was provide a simple act of kindness.

When she said nothing, he continued in the deep and sensual rumble she'd come to love whenever he spoke in a low, conversational voice. "I'm keeping you warm. Seems quite proper to me. The crime would be letting you shiver and freeze all night."

"Sorry," she whispered. "Lifelong lessons are hard to put behind you."

He chafed one hand up and down her bare arm. "If you're really wanting me to set you aside, lass, I will."

"No, it's silly. I…" He'd shown no interest beyond that night in the cabin when he crawled in beside her wearing only his smallclothes. And they'd been deliciously small, even if she had been too shy to appreciate the whole package exposed by him wearing such a miniscule piece of clothing. She sighed into the chilly air, fogging it with her breath. "Goodnight, Ramsay."

"Goodnight, Victoria."

Except sleep didn't come. No matter how she tried to will herself into slumber, rest remained elusive. The peaceful rhythm of his breaths suggested he'd already fallen asleep. Dim light filtered through the windows from the street lamps outside, providing the minimal amount she needed to see.

For a while, Victoria watched the shadows on the wall, but the flickering and imaginary shapes unsettled her, rather than soothing her to sleep. "Ramsay?" she whispered. "Are you awake?"

"I am."

"If it isn't too personal a question to ask, why don't you have a mate? If you're Father Bear, I would have expected you to have many little ones."

"I only claimed the title this past year. When we met, I was Little Bear."

"That still doesn't answer my question. Or is the Little Bear not allowed to have a family?"

A chuckle rumbled in his chest beneath her ear. "No, I could have had a family then if I desired one. The truth isn't scandalous or exciting. I simply haven't found a woman I wish to have at my side."

"Oh."

"What about you? Aren't noblewomen of your kingdom married by now?" His breath was warm against her hair and oddly comforting. "Not that I'd take you to be old. I only assume a woman old enough to travel on her own is a woman of marrying age."

"Father tried to arrange a marriage for me once. I declined the offer."

"Why?"

"I didn't want to marry a stranger," she answered simply. "When the time comes, I want to be able to choose my own husband. Someone I actually care about."

"But you've been with the queen for years, and you said yourself you traveled with Griogair. Did none of the wolves interest you?"

"Not in that way." She sighed. "Ana would say I'm too picky. And she would be correct. I find faults where none likely exist."

"Oh? So what faults would you say lie with me?"

She raised her head from his chest and frowned. "Really?"

"Yes. I'd love to know." He tucked a stray wisp of her disheveled blonde hair behind one ear, while his smoldering brown eyes pinned her beneath a gaze filled with seductive promise.

Victoria froze, her thoughts turning into mush.

Physically, Ramsay was as fine a specimen as they came. He hadn't removed his shirt to lie down for bed and still wore a loose linen tunic. The opening at the collar revealed soft, golden brown hair over a broad chest sculpted from hard muscle. And then there was the rest of him. She recalled green tattoos and silver ink against his bronzed skin.

"You're…" Victoria wet her lips and struggled to make her reflections gel into cohesive thoughts. "You are pushy at times. And overbearing."

"Overbearing," he mused.

"Very."

"Gentler than what I expected you to say."

"What did you expect?"

"You don't seem to like me much," he explained. "I imagined your words would include things like coarse, rough, and crude."

VIVIENNE SAVAGE

"A little of all of those things, but in a pleasant way."

"Oh?" He lifted a brow and she giggled at his confused scowl.

"Noblemen of Creag Morden are quite different. Their hands are soft and they know nothing of work. Depending on their station, they *may* know how to handle a sword, but not always," she explained. "So, while I do find you coarse and rough, it isn't an insult."

It was a delightful change from the barons, lords, and other men her father had been willing to gift her to like a lamb. At one point, there'd been a pretty foreign prince from across the sea, and then Anastasia had saved her, paying her bride-price and sweeping her away to freedom. Victoria sighed.

Ramsay snorted. "In Cairn Ocland, all are taught to wield a sword, plow, and line. Royals and commoners alike."

"I learned nothing until Griogair and his kinsmen taught me. For that, I will forever be grateful to him." She suppressed a shiver when the bear's fingers traveled down her spine.

"Surely the old wolf didn't teach you to pick a lock."

"I learned that on my own."

"And what does a princess need to pick locks for?"

"I'm not a princess, for one. As for the knowledge… I used to sneak out of my room." She laid her head back against his shoulder and smiled. "Which will be a story for another time. Goodnight, Ramsay."

Chapter 7

ICTORIA AWAKENED TO the bleak interior of the gnomish home without sunlight. From what she had discerned during their adventure, the lanterns in the city operated on a strange cycle, providing light for several hours before dimming. She sensed Ramsay's presence, his long body stretched alongside her, but couldn't see him.

Not that she needed her vision to know the impropriety taking place. At some point during their rest, she'd slid a thigh over his hip and buried her face against his throat to warm her cheeks.

And apparently Ramsay had decided to warm his hand by cupping her breast. His entire palm covered the modest swell with ease, reminding her of why a true lady wore a corset. Clothed in only a tunic and a thin layer of cloth wrapped around her bosom, she felt naked and yearned for the corset she'd abandoned at the start of her training.

But no, Griogair and the female werewolves had refused to allow her such comforts, claiming no woman could battle with full flexibility while hindered by whaleboning.

Without thick layers of lining and brocade to pad her body, her nipple tightened under his palm. He squeezed and mumbled something incoherent in the Oclander tongue, a language she knew with only minimal confidence. She preferred when he spoke Mordenian.

Instead of slapping his hand away, she waited, face feverish and heart hammering in her chest.

"Ramsay?"

He grumbled another low noise in his throat, a reverberating growl that vibrated against her cheek. Her core clenched and the muscles fluttered in response.

Human men never made those sounds. Neither had wolf men, though she'd wandered past more than a few couples stealing private time in the dark during the pack's campouts beneath the stars. They hadn't been shy about showing love to one another, open and free.

His calloused thumb rubbed across her nipple back and forth, jerking her attention back to the present. The pleasant friction brought heat coursing through her body and a desperate need to experience more.

As though he sensed her pending surrender, Ramsay shifted their positions, rolling her to her back without releasing her from his embrace. His scruffy cheek chafed against her throat and moved lower, stubble abrading her collarbone. Within seconds of him removing his hand, the heat of his mouth replaced the missing warmth. He suckled her nipple through her shirt and she arched beneath him in response.

Neither one spoke, for which she was grateful, worried that words would shatter the fragile moment.

The hand on her stomach moved again, sliding to her hip then down to her thigh where he traced the crease. Instead of clamping both legs together, Victoria parted them. Ramsay accepted the silent invitation and skimmed his palm down the front of her pants.

Each time he stroked her, a war took place between the demure training of her youth and the womanly desire flourishing within her now.

Ramsay plucked the strings lacing her breeches and drew them open. Beneath, she wore only thin white undergarments.

"Should I stop?" he asked against her breast.

With every touch, he scrambled her thoughts further until her brain became mush and she couldn't put together a coherent sentence. Her hips bucked upward when he breached the thin layer of cotton, and she moaned while pushing against his fingers. What he was doing should have been illegal. Sheer torture.

Having all the power in the world to stop him, Victoria said nothing.

"Should I stop?" Ramsay repeated.

"No."

"No man's ever done this for you before, has he?"

She shook her head in the dark, cheeks flushed. How could she possibly look into his face again after this?

After a long pause, Ramsay murmured, "It's nothing to be ashamed about, lass. Does it feel nice?"

"Yes," she gasped.

"Then stop feeling guilty and enjoy a moment for yourself for once," he whispered against her ear.

For all her efforts in private to bring herself pleasure, no attempt had ever tightened her body as much as Ramsay did. She squirmed and twisted before surrendering her body to him, half desperate for him to rip away her breeches completely.

He wound her muscles tight with the next glide until Victoria felt stretched to her limit. Heat surged over her entire body, and she hated her clothes for being between her and his talented hands.

Please, please, please, she begged silently when he shifted beside her onto his knees, only a hint of his silhouette visible to her human eyes.

Years of restraint crumbled the moment his lips touched where his fingers had been only moments before. Startled, she grabbed two handfuls of his blond curls while her cries echoed off the stone walls and low ceiling.

Hot and molten pleasure coursed through her like she'd never experienced before. She trembled and buried her toes against the thin layer of their makeshift pallet while gasping for each breath.

The moment carried her away on fierce waves of delight and mounting rapture, but it wasn't until Ramsay nuzzled his face against her throat that Victoria returned to her senses. Her chest heaved while she searched for words. The only ones to come to mind felt insufficient. Weak.

Ramsay seemed to sense her inner turmoil and kissed

her throat again. "No woman should go all her life without knowing pleasure."

If she'd known his fingers possessed even a tenth of the pleasure he'd shown her, she would have surrendered her misconceptions about virginity in the cabin. She melted and sighed his name as the tender kisses resumed.

"Go back to sleep for a little bit, lass. I'll fix up some food with what I can find."

How in the name of the gods did he expect her to sleep after that? She felt both exhausted and exhilarated, hyperaware of everything down to the rustling of his kilt when he rose and moved away. Quiet, she listened to his retreating footsteps.

Some time passed before Victoria crawled from the pallet, rose, and stretched her aching back. Since Ramsay had left the lantern, she shook it to activate the alchemical stones and investigated the house again. She found a small washroom with plumbing similar to the fountain outside. Forced to crouch on her knees, she filled the basin with a small amount of cold water and freshened up.

"If I wasn't awake before, I would be now," she muttered while donning her clothes again. If his fingers and mouth had brought such pleasure, what would it feel like to actually make love with him?

"Victoria!" his voice rumbled through the little home.

"Be right there!"

She straightened her clothes again after the chilly bird bath, mourning that the tiny basins were too small for a deep soak, the water too cold for a decent wash, and her supply of fresh clothing too limited to change as frequently as she wanted.

But isn't this what I asked for? A true adventure? There's no time for pedicures and rosewater baths while on an epic journey. This is what I wanted.

Gooseflesh prickled over her arms when she emerged to find Ramsay starting a fire in the narrow lane between the homes. He'd roasted the mushrooms he could identify as safe for a human to consume, and together they dined on those, dried meat, and the stale bread she'd baked in his cabin.

Despite her fears of changing the friendly but safe dynamic between them, Ramsay met her gaze without judgment or condemnation. He patted the space beside him on the mossy earth and offered a portion of the meal on a serving platter crafted from silver. In her hands, it resembled a fancy dinner plate instead.

"I've refilled our water skins too. Even after all this time, the gnomish piping doesn't appear to have rusted or corroded. It's undamaged. I've only seen such a contraption at Castle TalDrach. Never anywhere else."

"Do you wonder what my ancestors could have possibly done to kill them?"

"I do. Perhaps we'll discover the fate of the gnomes while we're here. It'll be a story for you to tell that niece of yours for sure."

Victoria flushed with pleasure. "Yes. It will be."

With no reason to clean up after themselves, they left the child-sized dishware behind and resumed their journey toward the center of the city. This time, Victoria had a plan to mark their progress and she used a rock to scrape notches across the cobbled paths.

As they reached the end of the lane and entered the city's next district, the architecture subtly changed and the single-story homes became vast and sprawling structures. A cluster of buildings with elegant, domed rooftops shone beneath lanterns.

Every contraption constructed by the gnomes had been built to last, even down to the lamps shining on each street corner. Dazzled, she wondered what energized the lights, how the power operated, and what mysteries could be removed by the king's adventurers and studied in depth to advance their kingdom.

"I believe that may be the king's palace. See how it shines. I'd bet you anything that's real gold leaf on the rooftop," she said. "See the stained glass in the windows? Unless it was crafted differently then, the color red is crafted with gold dust." She'd already decided, if the Gnome King were to live up to his reputation in the legends, then his palace would be the most ostentatious and elaborate of all the buildings in the city.

A stone gate with smooth, polished walls separated them from the other side. As they approached the gate, Victoria fantasized about Ramsay prying it open with his bare hands, forcing his biceps to bulge and sweat to sheen on his brow.

He disappointed her by touching one stone slab with his hands and applying his shifter's gift as a stonecrafter. It crumbled into harmless pebbles and they crossed into the courtyard, where a lavish world of extravagance awaited them.

"I thought you couldn't use your talents here?" Victoria asked.

"Do you see any runes? Apparently those protections only exist on the perimeter walls of the city to keep my ancestor kin out of the kingdom. That's my theory at least."

A walking path encrusted with gemstones led them to the palace doors. The remains of fallen guardsmen in full battle armor littered the subterranean courtyard. Inside was no less grand, a spectacle in noble metals. Gems hung from the ceiling and jeweled mosaics spanned across the walls. Gnomes didn't work in paint—they used polished stones to create masterpieces.

Unlike the rest of the tiny buildings, Ramsay walked tall beneath the vaulted ceilings with no danger of bumping his head. Normal-sized doors operated by lever systems made her wonder if the gnomes were fond of the open spaces, or if they'd once entertained human-sized guests.

"Everything here is normal size," she murmured.

"It is," Ramsay agreed. "All the better for a king to entertain foreigners. Although he stole children from the humans, I'm sure there was once a time when the monarchs before him made friends among the topside kingdoms."

Victoria stepped over a pile of bones held together in

white metal armor polished to a mirror shine once she swiped her thumb over the breast plate to clear the dust away. She crouched beside the deceased warrior and studied his weapon, a crossbow far too large for his small hands.

Before she could rise and move on, Ramsay knelt beside her and removed the weapon from its previous owner's dusty grip. "It appears to be a gnomish heavy crossbow. It would have taken two of them to draw the string, but..." His gaze dropped to the crank on the side, and then he turned it and a mechanism slowly drew the string. "Ah, there. Quite ingenious, isn't it? Even you could cock this weapon."

"I shouldn't, it belonged to the dead."

He snorted. "If you want it, keep it. Better in the hands of the living than the bones of the dead."

"You're right."

Since she'd left her crossbow with Safiyya for the woman's protection, she accepted the relic, and counted herself lucky fate had blessed her with a replacement. It fit right in her hands, as if made for her.

Would they need it? A cool trickle slid down her spine, and the fine hairs on her arms rose.

"We should continue now unless you've seen other corpses you want to rob," she teased him.

"Don't be so noble now, you were happy to sleep in a dead man's home," he quipped.

"Seriously though, Ramsay, I thought you Oclanders had more respect for the dead than this."

"We have more respect for our *own* dead than this. These gnomes aren't my countrymen."

"Oh."

Inside, they traveled beneath a lavish chandelier strung together from hundreds of crystals resembling liquid starlight, some in unique shapes and others like slender, semi-translucent blades throwing rainbows around the expansive rooms. It struck her as funny how some surfaces repelled dust and others didn't.

It must be magic, she mused while tracing her fingers over one of the marble pillars. They passed beyond another set of normal-sized doors and followed a red velvet carpet into the audience chamber.

"There!" Victoria cried. She pointed to the sole skeleton at the end of the enormous hall. A throne arose from the stone, bedecked by jewels and occupied by only a single lonely skeleton. The deceased gnome wore royal furs and a gilded crown. "We've found him."

She hurried forward with Ramsay on her heels, half afraid some latent trap would spring to life before she crossed the room. Nothing happened. The corpse didn't rise from the dead, and their movement failed to activate any kind of treacherous device.

Filled with pity, she examined the wee body and blinked away the burning sensation creeping beneath her eyelids. Abducting human children had been an inexcusable crime, but had every gnome, both young and old, deserved death?

What did such a thing to them? What force swept through an entire city, killing everyone in its path?

She wondered those things and more as she swept her eyes over the small skeleton. A ring shone beneath her lantern, gold and fitted with a single large ruby. Somehow it had remained upon the yellowed finger bone.

"That's it. That's the jinni stone we're looking for," Ramsay said.

"To be honest," she began in a quiet voice, barely a whisper, "I'm almost afraid to touch it. I've already set off one trap since our arrival, and I'd feel quite silly if we made it all this way for me to get us killed now."

"Use the cloth Safiyya gave you."

Victoria removed the folded square of fabric from her pouch and shook it out. The gold threads gleamed against the ivory cloth. Using it, she removed the ring from the skeletal finger and wrapped it tightly before shoving it back in the same leather bag. "Now we need to find the enchanted hammer, otherwise we can't free her husband from the lamp."

"Well it won't be here. We need to find a workshop." Ramsay took her by the elbow and guided her away.

"Do you know what a gnomish workshop looks like?"

"No idea," he replied in a cheerful voice.

Victoria eyed him, suspicious of his sudden enthusiasm. "You're surprisingly happy this evening."

"Am I? Must be the mushrooms."

After blinking in surprise a few times, Victoria pinched

herself. "Either I'm dreaming or you made a joke."

"I know how to joke, lass. I'm not always serious."

"You could have fooled me."

Chapter 8

A LADDIN HAD EVERYTHING a man could possibly desire, and still he wanted more. With his most recent wish, he'd requested his ifrit to create a map of every kingdom across the world, accurate down to the last stream and river.

He traced his fingers over the mountains and found their location, recognizing it for the lake nearby. With his first wish since reaching the backward nation of Creag Morden, he'd forced the djinn to create a defensible stronghold able to rival the sultan's palace in Samahara.

Yet it wasn't enough. He desired more.

His room was huge, lavish, and filled with splendor. Beautiful tapestries covered the walls, and rugs of Samaharan origin stretched across the marble floors. Gold gleamed on every candelabra, sconce, and fixture. He sat upon a throne cushioned with velvet beside a tiger stolen from the sultan's personal garden. Beside him, in a gilded cage, a rare phoenix from Liang fluffed its feathers.

Rumors had claimed it would sing, but the damned bird hadn't uttered a word or note of song since he'd claimed it from among the wizard's possessions. Disappointed, he stared at it. The phoenix stared back.

Stupid bird. "Perhaps I'll have you served up for dinner." He reckoned he could sell the feathers and make a fine bit of coin, but what good was more gold, when mountains of it were piled waist-high in every corner of his throne room. He had another chamber dedicated to treasure alone, and it gleamed with every type of polished jewel a man could desire.

Samiran had provided him everything, and yet he knew he hadn't tapped the ifrit's full potential. There had to be more.

"It's time to plan our next move," he muttered into the empty room. Taking the golden lamp from his belt, he rubbed his hand back and forth across its side.

"Samiran, come forth and grant me my request."

Crimson flame streamed upward from the lamp and coalesced into a masculine shape. Golden eyes gleamed from the flickering fire.

"What more could you possibly want?" Samiran asked. "I have given you a fortress and enough wealth to found a kingdom."

"Yes, but what good is a kingdom without peasants and citizens?" Aladdin asked. "Better yet, what good is a kingdom without a queen?"

"Why do you need more things you would only neglect and abandon?" the ifrit shot back.

Aladdin tipped his head back and stared at the floating figure beside him. The vein behind his temple throbbed, and a hot pulse of anger swept heat down his body. "You are mouthy for a creature bound to my service. Have you forgotten what happened last time you upset me?" he asked.

Samiran closed his eyes. "No, Master."

"Good. It would be wise for you to remember your place as my servant. If I require a conscience, I'll ask for it." Aladdin stroked the head of the tiger beside him and ruffled its fur.

"Very well. How may I serve, Master?"

"I have played at being a king long enough. I require a true kingdom and a queen to serve alongside me, but she must be a woman of true beauty with unmatched talent and royal heritage. No mere commoner will do."

"Such women are difficult to find, Master."

"Does this monarch have daughters?"

"One daughter."

"Go to her and present my interest. Bring her to me."

"I cannot."

Aladdin jerked his gaze up to the fiery spirit's face and studied him. "You are denying my wish?"

The stoic ifrit's neutral expression broke, eyes burning with the hatred the rest of his expression had failed to convey. "No. Merely unable to grant it, Master. His daughter is Queen Anastasia of Cairn Ocland, the kingdom to the north. Not only is she wed already, but she is of fae blood."

"So?"

"Her match to King Alistair of Ocland was personally arranged by Grand Fairy Eos years ago, and her marriage is protected by magical means equal to my own. To involve her in your strange machinations would be to grant her grandmother permission to interfere in your plans. To become eligible, Queen Anastasia must forsake her protection and come to you."

Damn. Aladdin settled back again. "Very well then. I will do as the sultan does and make a harem. Any woman I desire shall be mine."

"If that is your wish."

"In time, I want an empire. We will begin with these lands, while their king scurries to send men to—"

Rafa, his closest friend and second-in-command, rushed inside, most likely winded from the sprint up the hundred stairs to the castle's throne room. He was a huge man, the muscle behind their operation and partnership, and a native of Samahara unlike Aladdin. "We have a problem."

Aladdin leaned forward and raised his brows. "What happened?"

Rafa crossed the space between them with long strides and offered a rolled sheet of parchment. Whenever he split their band, they remained in contact by carrier hawk. "This news came from the south. Three of our men are dead."

"Three? Which?"

"The details are slim, but it appears Thirty-Nine was murdered by an act of sorcery. Thirty-Seven was mauled by an animal, and Forty was found with his throat slit."

"Sorcery?" Aladdin muttered while unrolling the message. He read over its contents and frowned. "Samiran, tell me who did this?"

"I cannot, Master. Their identities are shrouded in magic similar to mine."

"What are you saying? There's another ifrit in this forsaken kingdom?"

"Perhaps. Whatever it is, I can only speculate. I see darkness and fog in the distance, but I cannot grant the answer you seek."

"You test me, ifrit." Aladdin consulted the map beside him again, tracing his finger south until he located where he had divided the gang. "Question the townspeople in Rosegate. Perhaps they've grown bold and hired mercenaries."

"It's possible," Rafa said. He stroked the braided tip of his beard. "And if we determine they have?"

"Raze the village. Make a statement to the imbeciles of this kingdom. If I'm to take over as ruler, I want them to learn my rule will not be questioned."

Satisfied with his plans, Aladdin resumed petting the docile tiger beside him. He'd prove his father wrong and show he could be more than a jobless urchin and a thief. He would become a king.

Rafa grinned back at him. "Excellent. I'd hoped you would say as much. Your will shall be done, my friend." He bowed and hurried out the way he'd come.

"If it is another ifrit, you'll soon have company," Aladdin told Samiran. "With two of you in my control, no one will dare oppose me. Not even this Grand Fairy. Now, deliver the gold in this pouch to my mother."

"She will not take it."

Aladdin slammed a fist into the arm of the throne. "Then make her take it!" he yelled, spittle flying from his mouth.

Samiran smiled. "I cannot, Master. While I can take gold to her, I cannot force her to spend it."

Every time he thought of his mother living in squalor, Aladdin wondered if it would be better to bring her to his fortress instead. His mind drifted to the stinking tenement in the south side of Liang's Golden City and the single room he'd shared with six other children. They hadn't been his siblings in blood, but they'd been brothers to him. Youngsters who died of illness over the years as his poor mother and father took in orphans off the streets and struggled to provide for them while the royal family wore silk and dined on fine cuisine.

His mother deserved better in her sunset years, but he couldn't deny that proving her and his deceased father wrong had been a major driving factor. He *could* make a life out of stealing and most certainly *would* prosper. "Then find a way, Samiran. Find a way to provide the things she needs."

"You do not understand, Master. I have taken her meals, gold, and wealth beyond all compare, but your mother wants nothing to do with anything that comes from your hands. She gives the food to the poor and tosses the gold onto the street. She donates the gemstones to the temple to atone for your thievery." The ifrit's eyes sparked white-hot, glowing brighter than miniature stars. "She is ashamed of you."

"Stop."

Goldilocks & the Bear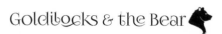

Samiran stopped for only a moment, and then he added, much like a petulant child, "She told me to tell you she no longer has a son."

Smoldering with fury, Aladdin jumped from the throne to his feet and swept the water kettle from the table beside it. "Stop. I told you to be silent!"

"You told me to stop. I did, for a time, and then I chose to relay a message. Does the truth hurt, mortal? Does it hurt to know your father died in disgrace, humiliated by your criminal ways? Does it hurt to know your mother lies hungry at this very moment as the fruit of your activities goes to waste?" Samiran leaned forward, emanating enough heat for sweat to bead on Aladdin's brow. "No matter the wealth I give you, nothing will take that away. No matter the wish I grant, you will always be the son who killed his own father with shame."

Shaking with rage, Aladdin poured water from the kettle into a stone basin. "Dip your hand inside."

"Punishing me won't change the truth."

"Dip your hand."

"You understand nothing of us, and I will be free one day. Perhaps not today, or tomorrow, but one day I will be free to watch you die," Samiran said in a quiet voice while lowering his hand toward the tranquil surface.

The water boiled and steamed. Like the previous times, Samiran made no sound, enduring the pain in silence. When Aladdin allowed him to remove his hand, a shallow inch of water remained and the creature's hand resembled a skeletal claw, all bone and no flesh or fire. It would regenerate in time. It always did.

"Return to the lamp. I'm finished with you for now."

He had a war to plan, after all, and he couldn't do that with a disobedient ifrit beside him.

Chapter 9

RELUCTANT TO SPEND another night in a small home where he risked knocking himself out if he jerked upright in the middle of the night, Ramsay argued for them to remain in the palace. Victoria agreed, but only if he cleared the bodies from the entrance hall.

Holding Victoria at night without anything more had become Ramsay's own personal hell. The memory of her whimpered cries and her taste haunted him, but he'd promised himself to do no more unless she took the first step.

According to the romantic novels he'd read based on Mordenian culture, brides only went to their marriage bed after being wed with their father's approval. And if that was what Victoria wanted, he could wait. He could wait until they arrived in Lorehaven, and he'd find this father of hers and plead his case. Prove he could be a worthy, dependable mate and an asset to their family.

But it was killing him to wait.

He rose before she stirred, to avoid further temptation. Victoria woke not long after and they shared a breakfast of fried mushrooms and hot oats sweetened with the jar of honey he'd brought along for the trip.

"I think I've eaten enough mushrooms for a lifetime," he grumbled. "I suggest we find the hammer and focus on getting out of here."

"For that to happen, we need to navigate away from the residential quarter to find wherever the gnomes did their handiwork. Look at what I found when I was exploring the side rooms." She laid an old, yellowed sheet of parchment across the stone table. It was brittle and tiny bits of the paper flaked off on the edges despite her gentle touch.

"You found a map."

"I did. And see here. I believe this is our location now. See the courtyard and the great wall surrounding the palace?"

"And if that's the palace, then this area here will be the residential district."

As he perused the map alongside her, he made out three distinct lower quarters of the gnomish city, with the palace occupying an oval-shaped upper section surrounded by buildings of equal beauty.

"I'd bet money, if we entered one of the adjacent structures, we'd find dead nobles in fancy clothing. This area of the city is a place for the wealthy."

Ramsay glanced at one of the remaining sections of the map. "We crossed through the fringe of their merchant quarter when we first entered the city, which makes sense, aye? If that's the way they bring in guests and visitors, they'll want tourists to see the goods and make purchases."

"With logic like that, it makes you wonder how well our

 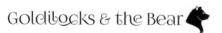

kingdoms worked together before the Gnome King began to conduct his raids."

"Or where he got such a fool idea in his head. A man doesn't come up with that kind of evil on his own, lass. My guess? Your ancestors may have given some of those children to the gnomes willingly at one point, but the supply didn't meet the demand."

"That's awful."

"That's life," he retorted.

"Not in Cairn Ocland."

"No." He gazed at her in quiet study. "Not in my homeland, but in others across the world, and in Safiyya's kingdom, I hear it's the norm."

"Not in Creag Morden. My ancestors wouldn't do that," she insisted.

Refusing to stir an argument over so inconsequential a subject as speculation about the past, Ramsay quieted and bent over the map again. "Here. I'd bet you this is where we'll find the engineers and metalworkers. It's close to the mines."

With their path planned and committed to memory, they emerged from the palace and made their way toward the mines. It didn't take long to find the remains of the first human, larger than the gnomes but too small to be an adult. Ramsay's disdain for the deceased ruler increased exponentially with each additional discovery.

"He was a monster," Victoria said sadly.

Although the mines loomed before them, they turned

into the engineering sector and made their way down the lane, passing cold forges on one side and workshops on the other. Signs proudly displayed painted images of gears and sprockets above some of the store windows. Windows displayed strange, unfamiliar contraptions, and stores held a bounty of goods operated by clockwork mechanisms.

But they found no special, magical tool in all the places they visited, until at last, disappointed and exhausted with their search, they gave up and started their way back toward the castle.

"There's nothing," Ramsay said. "I wonder if this hammer truly exists, or if it's a fable."

"Safiyya wouldn't send us below ground without just cause. It has to be—" Victoria abruptly stopped and peered past him.

"What?"

"I thought I saw something. A light. A violet light with a golden center, like fire. It flickered, but as soon as I focused on it, it vanished."

"Strange."

Before he could inquire further, Victoria took off at a jog down the narrow street. At the intersection of two lanes, they found the largest workshop of them all occupying the whole of the corner. The illegible gnomish letters had been spelled in glossy gold above the human-sized doors.

"This is it. I know it!" Victoria said.

Inside, they found an inventor's paradise beyond anything Ramsay's imagination could have dreamed up. Like most of the other buildings, the lights remained intact, and small spotlights shone upon marvels he hadn't noticed in other stores. To their left, a glass-fronted display featured miniature grandfather clocks set in faces smaller than Victoria's palm, each one attached to a delicate chain. Dead ahead and behind the proprietor's counter, gilded phoenixes crafted from gold and rubies shone like ornate statuettes.

"They're beautiful," Victoria breathed. She wiped her thumb over the top of the phoenix's crest, clearing dust away. The head bobbed slightly, revealing it was yet another mechanism with movable parts.

"They certainly are," he agreed.

The more they explored, the more the craftsmanship amazed them, and they hadn't even left the first room. Skill unlike anything he had ever seen aboveground awaited them in every corner of the shop until they ventured through a waist-high door behind the shopkeeper's counter.

Soon after ducking into the rear of the shop, they found the remains of the brilliant creator at a work table surrounded by tools. Lack of airflow gave the room a musty odor.

"There's an entire shelf of hammers." Victoria put her hands on her hips and huffed out an exasperated breath. "Which one is it?"

Ramsay checked the high shelves, which weren't particularly high considering the inhabitants of the city. A rolling ladder nearby would have given the gnomes access to the upper level of supplies. "We're looking for the one that feels like magic."

"Easy for you to say," she grumbled as she moved down the bottom shelf, examining each hammer in turn.

Nothing stood out, each one the same as the last.

"What about the cabinet over there?" Victoria asked, pointing across the room. "You check that while I search these drawers."

Ramsay crossed over and pulled open the wooden doors. More tools were within, but unlike the shelves with their unorganized arrangement, each item in the cabinet had been set in a specific place. Chisels and files laid on velvet cushions, nails made from scarlet metal filled glass jars, and mallets hung from hooks on the back wall. In the center, hung at the top, was a single hammer.

"I think this is the one." Ramsay lifted the hammer from its placement on the wall. Despite its small size, it was surprisingly heavy. The metal head shimmered with an ochre luster and tiny runes had been engraved into the enameled handle. An electric buzz vibrated against his fingertips.

"Are you certain?" Victoria asked. She abandoned her search and hurried over.

"Yes. This is it." He tied the hammer to his belt and stepped away from the cabinet.

"Well that wasn't so awful." She smiled up at him. "Now we just need to find a way out. Surely that can't be too hard a task, right?"

"Let us hope so," he replied.

They stepped out from the workshop into the street. Out of habit, Ramsay glanced up to look for the sun or moon, only to frown. He had no way to track the passage of time in the underground city.

"I can't wait to feel the sun again," Victoria murmured, echoing his thoughts.

"Maybe with the hammer I can break the runes at the entrance hindering my magic."

"I don't remember seeing any."

"They were faint and difficult to see, mere etchings against some of the marble pillars flanking the doors. You didn't exactly take the time to look around either."

The hopeful gleam returned to Victoria's eyes. "You're right. We can—"

Something clattered behind them, metal striking against metal. Ramsay raised a finger to his mouth and moved to the left, gesturing for Victoria to go the opposite way

If he hadn't seen the way she handled the bandit on the road, he would have been reluctant to part from her side at all. Whatever the wolves had taught her during her two-year sojourn among them, it had been enough to make her a capable woman with the skill to sneak up on a thief.

For the first time since their partnership began, Ramsay noticed Victoria walked with the soundless grace of the wolf clan's best hunters. He didn't see her either when he turned to find her, but he smelled her in the air. Human, fresh, and alive unlike the vast cemetery of gnomish bones surrounding them.

In the cramped streets dividing the engineering sector from the blacksmiths' quarter, a rank smell overpowered anything left of Victoria's sweet scent. The stink of sweat and filth invaded his nostrils and choked him long before he peered into the narrow aisle.

A cave troll crouched low and sniffed the ground, its eyes wild and feral. It had knocked over

While one experienced bear shifter could usually take on a mountain troll, their subterranean cousins were larger, hardier, and angrier, forced to thrive only by survival of the fittest in environments where food was scarce. The creature stood taller than Ramsay, covered in shaggy brown and black fur. Horns curled back from its prominent jaw and knife-blade claws scraped the ground when it walked. Roaring, it displayed rotting yellow teeth in its enormous maw, blasting the stench of its fetid breath down the street.

Its tremendous girth barely fit in the narrow lane, and it frequently brushed against obstacles and building faces while walking. Distracted, it paused alongside a corpse beneath one of the many street lamps. It snatched a femur out of the disintegrating cloth holding the rest of the skeleton together, then chewed the knobby joint on the end. Bone cracked. With so many dead bodies, it was no wonder the beast had wandered into the city. The whole underground kingdom must have looked like a buffet.

Suddenly, the troll's nostrils flared, and it drifted from the aged bones toward the street again. The creature raised its head and sniffed toward the direction Victoria had gone. Its lips curled back as it snarled and took two shambling steps forward before charging down the road.

It smelled her. Ramsay couldn't let allow it to sniff Victoria out, and if he was going to battle a creature as vicious as a troll, facing it with a sword would be suicide.

Unwilling to take the risk, Ramsay shifted and growled a challenge as he stepped out into the road. The troll spun around with a matching roar.

Standing on his hind legs as a bear brought Ramsay to the creature's chest height. While it had him matched when it came to size and weight, it couldn't meet his intelligence. The cave troll's bulk crashed into him, but Ramsay rolled with the momentum and hurled his assailant beneath him.

Snarling, they bit and snapped at each other, the adjacent structures a casualty of the enormous beings hurling each other down the street. A lantern pole bent beneath Ramsay's back and sent pain lancing across his spine.

A barbed crossbow bolt tore through the troll's shoulder. The bloodied tip had gone all the way through. Howling in rage and pain, the beast flung itself away from Ramsay and spun around, searching for its attacker. Another bolt whizzed through the air and struck the creature in the chest. Ramsay followed its path to Victoria, who had climbed onto the ledge of a taller two-story warehouse. She crouched on the roof and cranked up the crossbow, loading another bolt.

Before the troll could head after her, Ramsay lunged into

the creature's side and dragged his claws through the shaggy fur. Their fierce brawl began anew, beast against beast, tooth and claw. Two more bolts whistled through the open space, each one thudding into the troll's back. The beast staggered and Ramsay rushed forward, slamming it into a wall. In a desperate bid to free itself, the troll clamped its jaws down on Ramsay's shoulder. Their mingled roars echoed through the entire city.

Using the last of his strength, Ramsay slammed the beast against the wall once more.

A sharp crack preceded the troll's limp fall to the ground. It lay unmoving.

Ramsay staggered aside and fell to the ground, transforming from bear to human within seconds. The troll had bitten deep through the muscle and torn a tendon, introducing him to indescribable pain. He swore under his breath and let his head loll.

Victoria's safety was all that had mattered, though he became dimly aware of footsteps slapping against the stone pathway.

"Oh God, oh God, you're hurt." Victoria touched the jagged bite wound as blood spurt from it to the rhythm of his heartbeat. "There's so much blood. I don't know what to do. What do I do?"

"Nothin', lass. It'll heal."

"You'll bleed to death before it heals!"

"Then staunch it if it worries you so much."

He bit down on his tongue, refusing to admit how much the injury pained him. Victoria pulled bandages out from her pack and knelt beside him.

"I need to clean it," she babbled. "I don't have anything to clean it."

"It'll be fine. The bandages," he prompted.

She bound his wound, tying it off tightly enough to make him wince. Once the pain faded and the stars behind his eyes dimmed, he leaned back against the wall.

"Do you think the troll is what killed the gnomes?"

"I doubt it. A troll's life span is no more than fifteen or twenty years. These gnomes have been dead for centuries. Besides, trolls wouldn't explain the sudden deaths."

"No, I suppose they wouldn't." She settled down at his side and placed her hand against his forehead.

"What are you doing?"

"Checking for fever."

Ramsay snorted. "Surely you've come to know enough about shifters to know we don't sicken."

"That isn't true. When I lived with the werewolves, a trio of cubs fell very ill with cradle cough."

He chuckled at her and took both of her hands to lace their fingers, even though he could barely move his arm. "Regardless, even if I were human, you wouldn't find infection so soon after. I'll be fine."

"Fine, but we should still rest."

He closed his eyes and managed a faint smile. "On that

we're agreed."

Victoria unsnapped her pouch and removed her waterskin. "You should drink something too."

"If it will make you stop fussing." He accepted the waterskin and took a few sips, making sure he left enough for her. Water had been plentiful in the residential and market quadrants, but they had only passed one fountain today.

"Get a little sleep, Ramsay. I'll keep watch."

He didn't know how long passed while he dozed. It might have been minutes or hours. Victoria had moved away during that time. He made out her slim figure perched on a low wall.

"Victoria?"

"Good, you're awake." She hopped down and made her way over to him. "How do you feel?"

"As a man should when he's been pounded by a troll."

A fragile smile curved her lips. "Smartass."

"Better than the alternative." He stretched and rotated his arms. "I think I'm good now. You can take this off."

With reluctance in her worried gaze, Victoria unwound the bandages and looked beneath the linen. An angry puckered line stretched from his neck to his shoulder, crusted with a dried scab but no longer seeping blood.

"It's… the wound is closed."

"Mostly. It doesn't feel pretty yet, but as I said, I'll survive. The injury should be healed by tomorrow. For now, we had better get out of here. Where there's one troll, there are bound to be more. They're pack creatures."

"Pack creatures?"

"Aye. They live in packs of six to ten but hunt alone. When this one fails to return, others will come in his place, seeking him. We need to go."

"But where?"

"Easy. We follow the smell. That creature came inside somehow. That could be our way out."

Victoria shot him a skeptical look, but he smiled and rose.

"Do you need to, uh, smell him?" She gestured to the dead troll.

Ramsay chuckled. "No. I had a good whiff when we were up close."

They passed by the shaggy corpse and headed deeper into the work district. Now that he knew what to look for, it was easy to follow the troll's path due to the cracked bones and tufts of fur caught on the rough walls.

"Do you really think there are more of them?" Victoria asked in a whisper. She kept close to his side.

"Outside, more than likely, or they'd have come running the moment the fight began."

"Oh… I suppose that makes sense."

"My guess is that one wandered in through the mines. See?" He gestured ahead to a dark, square-cut tunnel entrance in the rock. It was small, barely large enough for a human child, exactly as Safiyya said.

"You won't fit in there. I'm not even sure I would." Victoria's steps slowed and worry shone in her blue eyes. "There's no way the troll came in this way. He was bigger than you, at least twice your height as a man."

"You're right. Which means there's another entrance somewhere. The stink of troll coming from inside is heavy."

"Maybe we should go back the way we came, as we planned earlier," Victoria pointed out.

"All right. If that fails, at least we have this as a backup plan. I'd still like to try and find where it came in, though. Make sure nothing else came with our furry friend."

They followed the cavern wall, passing ten more small mine entrances, until they came to a large crack. Ramsay ran his hands over the stone and leaned into the crevice, sniffing. The eye-watering smell of troll assaulted his nose, and dread raised the hairs on the back of his neck. The mines weren't a potential escape route for them to take after all.

"We need to go. Now."

"What's wrong?" Victoria asked.

He grabbed her wrist and tugged her away from the wall. "He wasn't alone after all. The smell is too strong for a single troll, which means either more are coming through the mines as we speak or—"

"They're already here," she finished.

His lips pressed together, mouth set in a grim line. "We need to get to the lift."

"But they'd only follow up the stairs."

"Then we have to hope we get there before they realize we're here."

A bellowing howl rose up from behind them. An answering call echoed from the other side of the city. The noise sent a chill racing down his spine.

He smelled them, coming closer and closer. The first shaggy beast slunk into view a moment later. A second one shuffled between two buildings and growled. Victoria gasped and edged in beside him.

"Ramsay, what do we do? There's too many…"

"Climb onto my back," he told her.

"Your back?"

"Yes, and hold on tight."

He shifted and nudged his enormous bulk into Victoria's side. At first, she made no move, eyes wide upon him, but then she seemed to understand his plan. She took two grips of his shaggy fur and vaulted atop him. Once he was certain she was secure, he took off at a run.

His claws scraped against the hard ground as he raced down the narrow gnomish streets and squeezed into the next corridor, heavily pursued by the trolls. He'd been wrong to assume there was only a pack of ten. They came in force, most likely lured by the promise of fresh meat.

Ramsay turned another corner while praying to the unseen stars above that he made it to the lift in time.

Natural wind didn't exist in the subterranean city, but Ramsay ran so quickly the air tossed back her hair. Her cloak flapped about behind her as the bear charged down the lane with the pack of trolls hot on his heels. Taking down one had been enough of a challenge, but six or seven—even at his best, they would have been destined for defeat.

Hard breaths whistled in and out of her lungs as she leaned over his immense withers. While cumbersome in appearance, the fierce beasts moved quickly once they lowered to all fours. Victoria stole a glance over her shoulder at their pursuers to see the trolls closing in.

Three stone pillars shot from the ground in great black spikes, pushing up through earth and the black pavement. One narrowly missed striking a troll, another was clipped in the side, and a third missed its mark entirely.

"Ramsay?"

He grunted and glanced back at her briefly.

"Do it again!"

He made another vocalization in his throat, a rumbling growl that would have been attractive under less life-threatening circumstances. Suddenly, she understood the attraction between her cousin and Alistair, loyalty and devotion aside.

Another stone skewer burst from the ground, spearing a troll through the shoulder. More of them appeared on the gnomish rooftops. They jumped from building to building, leaving ruin in their wake, crashing through ancient residences that had withstood centuries of time.

This was a place Anastasia would love to visit one day, a

 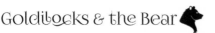

place to study and explore, and it hurt Victoria to see the filthy trolls laying waste to it. Maintaining a grip of Ramsay's fur with one hand, she drew the gnomish crossbow with the other.

I can do this.

Riding Ramsay became easier as she adapted to the bear's unusual gait. While it may have differed greatly from Rook's smooth rhythm, she felt no danger of toppling off. The bear growled in protest.

"They're gaining on us. I have to do something."

After swallowing down the nervous tension gripping her throat, Victoria hastily cranked the lever and drew the string taut again. The gnomes had taken all the difficulty out of the most common things, and it was easier this time than it had been on the rooftop, her hand accustomed to spinning the handle.

The moment she cocked it, another bolt sprang into place from an unseen reservoir in the machinery.

While Victoria may have regretted her failure to practice with the weapon when they found it, she certainly was relieved she'd allowed Ramsay to talk her into taking it. Squeezing the trigger in the nick of time, the bolt struck their lead pursuer in its throat.

Squeezing with her thighs, she remained atop Ramsay and thought back to the training Griogair had given her. Once, she'd thought it excessive. Now, their very survival depended on everything the wolf had ever taught her about keeping ahead of the enemy. From the pouch she wore fastened to her waist, she removed a small sachet of clinking, metal bits, caltrops that the wolves fancied when hunting larger game with soft, delicate feet.

She tossed a handful out behind them. The lead troll howled in pain and toppled over onto the sharp three-pronged spikes. The others used him as a step, crushing his body into the ground.

Another spry troll closed the distance after bounding over the caltrops left behind. As it soared through the air, twisting its hulking body toward them, it reached out to swipe at her with an enormous hand tipped by yellowed claws. His hot breath tousled her blonde hair.

She let the bolt fly. Through sheer luck, she struck the troll in the eye, and her would-be attacker fell back.

"Yes!"

Ramsay darted around the corner to the left, bringing the Gnome King's palace within view. The next turn brought them into the majestic courtyard with its platoon of skeletons.

The moment they crossed the palace threshold, Victoria leapt from astride the bear and pushed her weight against one massive door. Ramsay took the other side and used his furry paws to throw down the heavy bolt. Victoria pulled the lever jutting from the floor, and five additional steel bars shot across the doorframe in an alternating pattern. She'd seen similar set-ups in Castle Lorehaven's castle doors, making her wonder about the two kingdoms' past history.

When the first troll struck the door, the wood shuddered.

Its body collided again in an intimidating crash.

"Why did you bring us here?" she cried. "I thought we were going to the lift."

Ramsay rose onto two legs and adopted his human form again. "We had no time to make it, lass. The palace was closest, so I made a decision."

Victoria rubbed her face with both hands and cried out in frustration. It wasn't his fault. Neither of them had predicted the city would be overrun with opportunistic carnivores in search of a meal. "Can they break in?" she asked.

He paced in front of the door and eyed it, clenching and unclenching those enormous fists of his. "I doubt it. The big blighters are strong, but these are reinforced ironwood and built to last. They were meant to withstand an attack like this."

Despite his promises, Victoria hurried away when the doors trembled again. No matter how much the trolls hurled their bodies against the wooden slabs, they held firm.

Built to last indeed, she marveled while easing behind the large shifter. "Now what?"

"I don't know," Ramsay admitted. "At least this will buy us some time before they realize there are enormous windows. Maybe the Gnome King had an alternate route of escape."

Victoria considered the idea and nodded slowly. "In Lorehaven, King Morgan has a secret passage that leads out through the undercroft. Even Benthwaite has hidden corridors."

"Then we should start looking."

Another booming thud struck against the doors, providing all the encouragement she needed to abandon the castle's foyer and proceed forward into the next hall. Scouring every inch, Victoria searched the opulent setting while comparing it to the castles she knew best. She looked for anything out of the ordinary, testing the sconces for hidden latches and feeling around the doorframes.

"Anything?" Ramsay asked.

"No. Perhaps the throne room? One of my uncle's most accessible exits is behind his throne," she said.

"There's nothing in that bloody throne room but moldy skeletons," he muttered.

Lacking any alternate plan, they hurried into the throne room. Her heart slammed in her chest, pulsing too quickly for her to breathe. What if the doors didn't hold? What if the trolls overcame it through starved desperation?

They wouldn't. She had to trust in him, after all. The beasts were determined but dumb, and she doubted they'd realize the fragile high windows provided an easier entrance. Well, she prayed they wouldn't notice.

She hurried to the oil paintings to feel around each gilded frame. When she found nothing there, she turned to find Ramsay staring at her with a raised brow.

"What *are* you doing?"

"I'm trying to find hidden buttons."

"Griogair taught you such things?"

"He did. He told me one never knows when knowledge will

come in handy. That sometimes your ancestors hid precious objects in that manner back when all of the clan leaders and chiefs dwelled in actual cities." She found something cold and knobby jutting up from atop a portrait of a female gnome wearing lace and frills in a field of colorful mushrooms. Victoria heard a grinding noise, the sound of stone sliding against stone.

Ramsay whirled and reached for his sword. "What was that?"

"I don't know." Nothing in the room had changed that she could see. Wary of disabling the steel braces securing the castle doors, she peeked into the hall and counted all five had remained in place. "Nothing appears unusual," she muttered.

"Well, I don't see anything."

Except they had both heard the odd noise, and it had come from nearby. Bewildered, Victoria turned in a full circle, coming to a stop when her gaze fell on the throne. "No... something is different there," she muttered.

"No there isn't. It's the same dead git on his garish chair," Ramsay disagreed.

She shot him a dirty look and proceeded to the throne anyway. After circling around the gaudy creation of stone, gold, and metal, it occurred to her that the bottom of his robes had been disturbed, and they jutted out by a few inches.

"Strange," Victoria murmured. She crouched beside it and brushed aside the deceased king's hemline to reveal they had obscured an open drawer. While the refined fabric had withstood the test of time without rotting like some of the commoners' garments outside, dust puffed up from it. She coughed a few times into her shoulder then squinted to see inside the compartment.

Gold thread and sapphires glittered from within. "What's this?" She lifted it from the hiding place and offered the metallic length of fabric to Ramsay.

"Looks like a sash or belt of some sort." Ramsay brushed aside the dirt dulling the gemstones then passed it back to Victoria. "Keep it."

"I couldn't."

"Why not? No one here is using it, and the color suits you. Let there be something good we take out of this forsaken deathtrap. Besides, you were the one with the intuition that led to finding it, even if it isn't our way out of the city."

Victoria considered his words then wrapped the sash around her waist. Perhaps the Gnome King had been portly in life, because the accessory fit her slender middle with an inch to spare, as if made for her. Ramsay buckled it behind her back, but his hands lingered on her hips afterward.

He could have touched all his fingers together, not because she was so small and willow thin, but because he towered above her by at least a foot or more and had the largest hands she'd ever seen on a man.

"Perfect." His breath disturbed her hair. "If we weren't at risk of becoming a meal in the next moment, I'd take the time to admire you, lass. Now c'mon. There has to be another way out."

"Ramsay, I don't think there *is* a way out. What if we're stuck here for days without food and water while those beasts prowl below? We don't have supplies for that."

His deep growl ran a shiver down her back and covered her arms with goose bumps. "We do. We'll wait them out if we must. If we take care with the rations we have, we could survive a few weeks at the least. There's running water, and we aren't mounting a defense against intelligent humans capable of clogging the pipes. Safiyya is wise enough to seek help if we don't emerge in a few days."

The air returned to her lungs, the narrow pin hole that had been her windpipe, loosened enough for her to breathe. "You're right. Then in the meantime, I suggest we learn our surroundings and explore whatever remains of this castle. The ceilings are high, and while it may be a bit of a squeeze for you to enter most doorways, you shouldn't strike your head this time."

Ramsay frowned. "That hurt."

"I know it did."

The symmetrical throne room had a door on either side, so they chose the one on the left. Ramsay ducked behind her through the thigh-high doorway to enter a corridor with a raised ceiling that must have felt enormous to the gnomes who dwelled in the castle. Less than an inch of clearance remained between the top of Ramsay's head and the ceiling.

"The art is beautiful," Victoria murmured. "Look at the

paintings."

"No different from the ones in the throne room and the rest of the palace."

Victoria rolled her eyes at him and opened each little door along the way for a peek inside. Stairs at the end led to an upper level with a distinct difference in decor. She admired the carpets in shades of tranquil turquoise and stepped over a body dressed in dull browns and tans. Her imagination created a story for the nameless gnome, a servant in the midst of cleaning whenever the calamity hit.

"More dead," Ramsay muttered as he helped her by opening doors on the other side of the hall. He crouched down and peered through the threshold. "Bedrooms. We must be in the palace residence now."

"More stairs. Let's go up another level."

Her grumpy bear muttered under his breath and followed her up. They passed through a doorway into a larger hall.

"It occurs to me that the trolls may not be able to follow even if they breach the doors. They're enormous." Victoria peered back over her shoulder at Ramsay. "You barely squeezed your shoulders through some of those doors."

"You're right."

One room after the next, they found beautiful galleries with exquisite gnomish crafts and visions of art, some of which Ramsay convinced her to take for posterity. After all, who could tell their friends and family of their adventures into an underground ruin without proof from the journey?

As they wandered the gallery and stepped through another pair of doors into the next hallway, Victoria saw a pair of doors marked with crossed swords above them.

That's unusual.

After raising the bar and turning the lock, she opened one door and glanced outside. It would have resembled an ordinary balcony if not for the mounted ballistas and catapults affixed to it with heavy metal bolts. The balcony extended out of view and turned a corner toward the front of the castle and made her wonder if she'd be able to spy on the trolls down below.

Awestruck, she held onto the doorframe and tested the terrace with her weight. It held without creaking, appearing to be as stable as the rest of the castle.

Huge machines with sealed pots occupied the ledge, with miniature coal furnaces beneath them. She studied one curiously then touched the heavy pot. One nudge tipped it forward and sloshed the liquid contents concealed by its sturdy lid.

It had to be oil. Hot oil for dropping on enemies below. "Ramsay! Come look at this!"

"Come look at wh—what in the name of the stars are you doing, woman?" his horrified voice reached her.

"What does it look like I'm doing? I'm having a look outside."

"Come in from there, Goldi. Although we're about six stories up, it isn't much considering how short the wee lads made each level."

Goldi? She didn't question his choice of nickname, even if it did send a pleasant surge of heat through her body and create a flutter in her chest. "This is amazing. Look! Why didn't we notice these while outside and approaching the castle?"

"Why would we have noticed them?" Ramsay countered. "Neither of us cared to look up when we visited the first time, or again when we fled the trolls to take refuge inside."

"Good point. Well, I'm going to have a look at the trolls."

When Victoria took a step, Ramsay panicked and grasped after her. His fingers grazed her arm but missed when she danced beyond his reach.

"Don't you dare walk down that balcony."

"Why not?"

"What if they see you?"

The corner of her mouth quirked. "We're at least forty or more feet in the air. I doubt they'll leap that high." She glanced at one of the gnomish battle stations. "I wonder if these work."

Ramsay didn't answer her, but when she glanced behind her over her shoulder, she saw the massive bear shifter standing on the ledge and gazing down at the world below. He clutched the stone molding with his enormous, white-knuckled right hand.

"You're coming with me?"

"Who else is going to make sure you're not snatched by a jumping- troll?" he shot back in a growl.

Victoria grinned, touched that he cared enough to face his phobia for the sake of keeping her safe, although she wondered if some of the concern stemmed from fear of losing the ring if he couldn't retrieve it from her corpse. Around the corner, they discovered multiple battle stations, also unchanged by the passage of time, aside from a heavy layer of dust on each metal surface.

"Whatever this metal is, it isn't iron," Ramsay muttered as he hunkered down to inspect a contraption. He brushed aside the remains of a gnome in the small seat, and then he took ahold of the weapon and aimed it below, peering down the sights. "Not a speck of rust or tarnish on any of the javelins. Aside from the dust, they're all as shiny today as they must have been the day the gnomes forged them."

"Intriguing, isn't it? But wouldn't you like to *try* one?"

Victoria glanced over the ledge at the assembly of trolls down below. One of them paced back and forth in front of the palace doors. Without warning, he charged full speed into the reinforced ironwood and crashed into it.

Ramsay flinched at the crash, but then he shot her a grin. "Perhaps I would. They won't be able to breach it for some time, if they're able to break through at all. We could certainly thin their numbers if any of these weapons remain operational," he mused.

"Certainly. Do you know how to work one?"

"It seems simple enough. I imagine some sort of burning agent or alchemical fire heats the oil. And the ballista is no different than what we fire today."

The Gnome King struck her as both paranoid and brilliant.

Had he anticipated some kind of war? Had there been battles in the undercity before in the past, inspiring him to have his inventors design such fancies and tools? She wanted to know more and mourned her inability to read the language, since they'd passed a library filled with tiny books.

I'll take a few with me. Anastasia is a talented linguist. If anyone has a chance at deciphering old gnomish text, it'll be her.

It was also the perfect souvenir gift for her dear cousin. Smiling, Victoria turned to face the castle and found another door carved into the stone.

"They were expecting trouble at the time of their deaths," she said. "This door isn't locked like the others, see? And there are other gnomes along the ledge."

"Perhaps on their way to take their places at the stations," Ramsay said.

"Yes."

"Great. I'm glad that's settled," the bear shifter said before squeezing his way inside the castle through a small door no taller than his waist level. "Now would you mind stepping away from your potential doom and onto safe, stable floor again?"

Chuckling, Victoria followed him inside.

Chapter 10

W HILE KEEPING WATCH on the progress of the trolls, Victoria's mind wandered to old lessons of training alongside Griogair. Not only had he taken her under his wing for the two years she'd lived among them, but he'd come and visited her frequently afterward to keep her on her toes. And sometimes she'd gone out with the wolves on hunts or to visit Sorcha and Conall TalWolthe, who were as much family to her as Anastasia, her flesh and blood.

There was no limit to Victoria's appreciation and respect for Sorcha, a woman who had chosen to live permanently among the wolves after mounting an impossible rescue against a powerful fairy queen. The huntress had saved an entire kingdom.

And then there was Ana, who had defended Castle TalDrach against the Dalbrovian army with only a small group of warriors and Alistair beside her.

More than anything, Victoria wanted to be like both of those women.

Down below, one of the trolls attempted to scale the castle wall again. For reasons she didn't understand, facing off against monstrous creatures eager to devour them was easier than battling another person. Glad that they had decided to start a fire beneath the pots before starting their vigil, Victoria stepped up to an oil boiler and cranked the lever, tipping the enormous cauldron. Its contents splashed over the troll, and the monster fell away with an earth-shattering roar of pain. The nauseating stench of sizzling skin and oil wafted up to her.

Bile rose in her throat. She swallowed it down and stepped back, too sick to observe the results but desperate to retain her composure.

Inside, Ramsay raised his furry head, shaken out of his drowse by the faint vibration.

"Go back to sleep," she called from the ledge.

For as long as the gates held firm and the trolls had no other way to breach the castle defenses, they had decided it was best if one slept while the other kept watch. Ramsay had taken the first shift while Victoria had a brief catnap, and now he sprawled on the ground in his intimidating bear form.

Moments later, his heavy body went slack again, and the subtle snores reached her ears. Victoria grinned.

While he slept, she nibbled some of the traveler's bread from their supplies and had a bite of jerky. She drank water replenished from the palace's well and let her mind wander to days long past.

Griogair would be proud, and thinking of him brought to mind her first lesson with the crossbow.

"Don't close one eye to aim, lass. Keep both open. Steady

your aim… take your time. Don't hold your breath so long. You'll get dizzy."

Victoria dragged in a deep breath and let it spill from her lungs again, alleviating the unpleasant burn. I want to do this. I want to do this. *She repeated it over and over in her head while lining up her shot.*

Her father's words bounced into her thoughts. "Don't look to us to take you in again when Anastasia tires of you. And she will. By the time it happens, young Prince Joren will have found another bride."

As she released the string, she saw her father's gloating face, saw her silent, discouraging mother. The arrow sliced through the air and landed true, striking directly left of the bullseye.

Beside her, Griogair raised both of his bushy brows, and then he set a hand on her shoulder. "You're improving well, lass. I remember when you couldn't hit even the edge of the target. You're getting better."

"I am?"

"Aye, now the real test begins. Can you do the same thing while mounted atop your horse?"

She stared at him.

"Without the saddle," *he added.*

"No, of course not. A lady doesn't—"

"I thought a lady was the very thing you didn't want to be any longer," *Griogair said.* "Or have you changed your mind."

Victoria tucked her chin and bit her lip as she considered the implications. Could she even remain on a horse bareback?

  VIVIENNE SAVAGE

"I... all right."

Of course, over a week had passed before she remained mounted while shooting, and even longer before her aim improved. Hitting the troll hadn't been mere luck, and calling it anything less than skill would be a disservice to her hard work.

The trolls grew too quiet for her comfort. Daring to peer over the edge again, she counted only seven of them beside the oil-scalded corpse. Earlier, she and Ramsay had each lessened their numbers by one after loading the ballistas and catching two of the beasts by surprise. One perished right away, taken by a javelin to the chest, but the survivor had loped away to hopefully die.

Where have the others gone? What are they up to?

Refusing to hope that a group of them had given up the chase, she crept along the ledge and glanced down below. Instead of scaling the palace, the trolls had stacked stones and gnomish armor against the garden wall while their hairy cohorts ran a diversion. They'd made it over the rear wall.

Glass shattered somewhere in the distance, beyond her sight.

"Ramsay!" Victoria cried. "I think they've found the windows!"

At first, she'd been positive they would be safe, but then she recalled the human-sized doorways. If Ramsay could fit, a determined, starving troll could squeeze through in a pinch on its hands and knees. And if they were smart enough to distract her with phony attempts to scale the palace, they'd be clever enough to find a way up.

With her heart in her throat, she dashed into the corridor and slammed the door shut behind her as the rousing bear shifter returned to his two-legged body.

"Then we have no time to waste. We'll have to try to make it past them to the lift."

"And if that fails?"

"Summon the damned jinni in that ring and hope for the best. If he screws us over, he has only centuries more in this city to look forward to."

Together, they sprinted to the end of the corridor and down a level, unable to descend farther to the lowest floor. Whether through eccentric design or accident, the deceased king's palace created a deadly maze, and Victoria couldn't remember their location to retrace their steps.

The first troll appeared at the end of the hall, too enormous to stand upright. It moved on all fours and sniffed the air, resembling a hound on the scent trail. Bright scarlet blood dripped from several gashes to its chest. It must have been the one to shatter the window and scurry inside.

Victoria ducked beneath a small doorway into a gallery of portraits and elegant oil paintings. Once Ramsay squeezed in behind her, he slammed the door shut and they rushed into the next room as the troll smashed through behind them. Due to its bulk and superior strength, it didn't need doors—

VIVIENNE SAVAGE

it crashed through the frames, creating its own. Hot on their heels, it pursued the pair into the next hall.

A second, smaller troll approached from the other direction.

It could have only been a troll juvenile, lacking the powerful muscle and dense bone of an adult. Slavering and grunting, it raced toward them as Ramsay charged into the lead on two legs. He dove forward, transformed in midair, and bowled through the beast, his bulk crushing it against the intersecting corridor's wall. Bone crunched, and it squealed sharply in pain.

"This way!" Ramsay cried, a man again in the next second before the troll's body even slumped to the ground. Blood dripped down his chest where he'd been gored by the young troll's horn.

Leaving a trail of caltrops behind them worked to slow the pursuing troll down, her success apparent when agonized bellows followed down the mazelike palace hallways.

"We'll never find a way out past them!"

"We will! Don't lose faith yet, lass."

Despair wove a tight net around her heart, clamping down until tears moistened the corners of her eyes. "I want to be back with Safiyya. I'm done with this adventure. I want to be outside again in the fresh air where we were before we came into this goddamned cave."

The breath squeezed out of her lungs all at once, compressing her from throat to middle. Something yanked her with the force of a ballista bolt hurtling through the air, and then she suddenly stood beneath the waning sunlight with warmth against her skin and the spring breeze against her sweat-dampened brow.

Beside her, Ramsay looked equally as confused. "What happened?"

Victoria released the handful of his kilt she'd knotted in her fist. "I... I don't know. I didn't use the jinni." She didn't even know how to summon the damned creature from his bondage.

"Well, that was quite the entrance." Safiyya stared at them from her bedroll where she lay reading a book. Rook and Dunn nickered from a few feet away, both horses tethered to a stalagmite.

"What...what happened?" Victoria twisted around. "We were inside the gnome castle, the trolls had crashed through, and then... I can't explain it."

Grunting with exertion, Safiyya pushed up from her makeshift bed. Her old joints creaked and popped in protest. "What's that around your waist, Victoria?"

"This?" She looked down to the jeweled belt. "A treasure from the throne room. Why?"

"Because I sense magic from it, child. May I see it?"

Trusting Safiyya with her newfound trinket, Victoria unhooked the sash and passed it over for her examination.

"What? You think this is how we made our miraculous escape?" Ramsay asked. He sat down heavily on the ground and then flopped onto his side against the cool, mossy ground. A ragged tear in his linen shirt revealed the deep puncture from the young troll's horn, although Victoria knew better than to fret again. In a few moments, it would be gone, leaving a faint scar in its place beneath a drying smear of blood.

"Possibly. The throne room, you said?" Safiyya glanced to Victoria.

"Yes."

After tracing one weathered hand over the gem-studded belt, Safiyya returned the dazzling sash to Victoria. "This would be the Gnome King's magic belt. As you were the one to discover it, it is only fitting if you keep it."

"But I don't… what does it even do?"

"It transports the holder anywhere they desire. You managed to activate it."

"Then… we can use it to travel to Lorehaven!"

"I'm afraid not, dearie. It's been depleted of much magical energy. It will need recharging before it can be of any use to us again."

Victoria stared at the belt in wonder. The sapphires winked in the pale light, appearing dulled. "Do you know how to activate it?"

"What were you doing before you disappeared?"

"Fleeing from trolls!"

"Aside from that," the old woman said.

"You made a wish," Ramsay said. "You wanted to be back with Safiyya."

"Interesting," the old sorceress murmured. "So it has similar properties to a jinni wish. You stated your desired location and here you are."

"How long do you think it will take to recharge?"

"There's no way to say for certain," Safiyya replied. "We'll keep an eye on it."

"Can it do anything else?"

Safiyya chuckled. "My dear, you seem to expect me to be a bastion of knowledge about obscure magical relics."

"You *were* a lorekeeper in a mage's tower."

"Ah, point made. Well, one story claimed it could conjure up a box of chocolate on demand."

"Chocolate." Victoria stared, wondering if the older woman was having a joke at her expense.

"So said the story. I think that's rather a wasteful use of magic, however, but you're welcome to try once the belt has recharged. The typical magic item recharges after a few days, but it could be weeks, and only time will tell."

"I think I'll save it for a more useful task."

"A wise decision. Now that the matter of the belt is settled, were you both successful in your task?" Safiyya asked. Her violet eyes, a rare shade Victoria had never seen in Creag Morden or Cairn Ocland, shone with hope.

Victoria removed the hammer from her bag and offered it to the sorceress. "Yes, although the strangest thing happened. We saw a light. An unusual light guided us to it."

"You saw a light." Ramsay grunted. "I saw nothing.

  Vivienne Savage

Anyway, if it's all right with the two of you, I say we remain here for the night and set out in the morning."

Safiyya tucked the hammer away. "Thank you for this, and I agree. You've both endured enough hardship and deserve the rest."

"But the trolls." Victoria looked over her shoulder.

"They're trapped. At least from coming through this way. I have no idea where the mines let out, but I don't imagine it's close," he replied. "We're better off getting proper rest."

Victoria recognized the wisdom in his words, but her pulse still raced from their close call. Ramsay held out his hand to her, and when she took it, drew her down beside him.

"We're safe now," he whispered against her hair. "Sleep. Everything will be better after some sleep."

Reassured by the confidence in his words and the comfort of his arms around her, Victoria closed her eyes.

Chapter 11

THEY AWAKENED TO a miserable dawn, the start of a cold and drizzling day. Ramsay had already left Victoria's side, and she found him outside the cavern perched upon the edge of a large stone. Lacking a fishing pole, he swept fish from the stream with his enormous claws. Although he didn't seem to mind the weather, Victoria hurried into her cloak and drew the hood. A single drop of rain reminded her of days spent abed as a child.

Safiyya still hadn't stirred.

She's weaker each day. Will she even survive the remainder of the journey to Lorehaven?

As if sensing the dismal thoughts about her declining health, Safiyya emerged from the cavern. Ramsay chuffed a cute, ursine greeting at the both of them and batted another fish from the water. Its slick body bounced and flopped against the slippery river rocks.

Safiyya smiled at him. "Good morning to you too, Ramsay."

"Good morning," Victoria agreed. While it was gray and chilly, it was still a morning worth appreciating.

Standing alongside Ramsay, she'd survived impossible odds.

The old woman tilted her face up to the bleak sky, a somber expression on her wrinkled face. "I suppose after so long underground, you must have hoped to see sunshine and clear skies."

"I did hope to see sunshine, but to be honest, seeing another day is good enough. Oh, here." Victoria pulled out the cloth-wrapped ring from her pack and offered it to Safiyya. "I was so tired yesterday I forgot to give this to you."

"I had faith you found it and didn't think it important enough to ask you about. Not after what you'd recently been through." Safiyya reached for the ring but hesitated, her fingers hovering over the golden band.

"Are you all right?"

"Yes, my dear. It's only that I'm so close now to freeing Samiran, I suppose I'm a little afraid."

"We're here to help you. Remember that."

Safiyya smiled then picked the ring up and rubbed her thumb across the embedded jewel. "Maziar, I call upon you."

A fine white mist streamed up from the gemstone. Victoria stumbled back a step and raised a hand to her chest, unprepared for the spectacle of a masculine shape coalescing from the mystic fog. When it faded, a man dressed in a garish display of colored silks remained. He was dark skinned, like unfired clay, a definite contrast to his pastel pink and turquoise garb. She blinked, trying to make sense of his unusual wardrobe.

"All this time you have known of my whereabouts, and yet only now do you come to find me." The jinni pouted and

 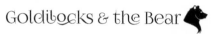

tossed his long braid over his shoulder.

"You were bound as punishment, Maziar. It was not my place, nor that of my mother or hers before her, to free you from your sentence."

"Yet here you are."

"Here I am. Tell me, how many wishes do you have left before you have made atonement for your crimes?"

"Crimes? I did nothing wrong."

"Queen Yasmina seems to believe otherwise."

"You care for her as little as you care for me. Do you think me a fool? I may have spent centuries trapped within that prison, but I know there is no love lost between you and your husband's sister."

"That has no bearing on this. I am in this land to free Samiran, but I require your help."

"You have only to command me. After all, you now control my ring."

"Yes, but it's my hope you would help willingly."

His eyes narrowed. "And why would I do that?"

"Because your lack of answer regarding how many wishes you must fulfill tells me Yasmina put an impossible number upon you."

Maziar frowned and said nothing, but Victoria was certain she saw a curl of smoke come out of his ear.

"If you help us free Samiran, as her brother, he will have the power to free you in return."

The jinni's eyes lit up, flaring with golden light. "Your

word on this?

"You have it."

"Then what is it you wish?"

"Can he magic us to Lorehaven?" Ramsay asked, wiggling his fingers as if casting a spell.

Maziar looked at him and frowned, disapproval etched in every line of his hard face. "No. A group of your size is far beyond my level of power."

"Oh."

"Then I ask that you see no harm come to us on the road," Safiyya said. "Turn negative, hostile, and aggressive attention away from us whenever it is within the limits of your ability."

"Your wish is granted," Maziar said. "Is that all?"

"For now, yes. Thank you."

Once the jinni retreated to the ring, an awkward silence fell between them. Safiyya dipped her head forward and closed her eyes, defeat adding further weight to her haggard features.

When she couldn't take more of the silence, Victoria touched the sorceress's shoulder. "Who's Queen Yasmina? And why does she despise you?"

"She is the Queen of the Ifrit, the most powerful and dangerous among the jinn."

"And Samiran is her brother."

Safiyya nodded. "Yes. She did not approve of our marriage or the son we conceived."

"You haven't spoken much about your son."

Since the start of their travel together, Victoria had

 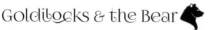

admired their companion's violet eyes. Three days apart from them had changed the vibrant hue, and now they were hidden behind milky cataracts. "Joaidane. We named him Joaidane, although I wonder if he remembers it at all, thanks to a curse Yasmina cast upon him as well." Before Victoria could say anything, she raised her hand and continued. "Like Maziar, he was deserving at the time, and he has since atoned. My only regrets are that I failed him as a mother, and that I have not had the chance to tell him in person how proud I am of the man he has become."

"Don't talk like that. We'll rescue Samiran and then you'll go home to your son."

"Ah, you have such a beautiful soul to say such things, but… no. My final days are upon me, child. I wouldn't live to make the return trip, even with Samiran. This quest across your kingdom is my last great adventure. I know that now."

The resigned, sad look in Safiyya's eyes broke Victoria's heart. Without thought, she hugged the older woman close. "I promise, I'll do whatever I can to reunite you with Samiran, even if it is for the last time. Between your ifrit and this belt, you'll get home to your son."

They left the ravine and rode throughout the day to put as much distance between them and the gnomish city as they could. Victoria didn't relax until they were hours and miles away.

She never wanted to encounter a troll again.

By sunset they'd set up camp in a thinly wooded forest.

Tired from their hard day of riding, they enjoyed a simple stew cooked over the campfire then went right to their bedrolls. Safiyya fell asleep in an instant, and Ramsay's quiet snores started up soon after, but Victoria found no peace.

As she sprawled beneath the stars, she wondered whether her parents would be happy to see her, and if they were worth her time at all.

Her father's final words to her had become a sorrowful mantra, despite her best efforts to clear them from her mind. She'd disappointed them by turning aside the perfect marriage prospect, a magic-wielding prince from a small but wealthy nation known for its unusual winter vineyards and sweet ice wines.

If she had married Prince Joren, she would have brought immense honor to the family. By refusing him, not only had she ruined her father's chances at claiming a queen for a daughter, but she'd cast aside the only eligible bachelor in all the northern kingdoms.

Why do I even care what they think?

The answer wiggled into her subconscious and clenched her throat as unshed tears burned beneath her lids. *Because I love them. Even though they hurt me, I love them dearly.*

Because she hadn't seen her mother in nine years, missed tea with her Aunt Lorelai, and longed for watching sports in the arena on a fine autumn day. For years, spectating the knights at their showmanship had been a favorite activity for her and Anastasia. It probably wouldn't be the same without her cousin.

The sheets to her left rustled noisily as Ramsay shifted onto an elbow. While they had plenty of room in the camp, the bear shifter had laid out his bedroll beside hers. "Goldi?"

"Yes?"

"Are you all right?"

"Yes." Her throat tightened again.

"Far from it, I'd say. What's wrong?"

Refusing to let her voice betray her again, Victoria rolled onto her side and placed her back to him, tugging the blanket up tighter around her shoulders. It didn't work. Ramsay loomed above her and placed his enormous hand on her arm. The warmth of his touch penetrated through her clothing like a brand, imparting heat and comfort she wished he could wrap all around her instead.

"Whatever it is… I have a good ear, if ever you feel the need to speak."

The floodgates opened. Despite her desire to be stoic and strong, the tears flowed freely onto the cushion beneath her head.

"It's silly," she whispered, afraid of awaking Safiyya. The old woman moved more slowly each day, and when they roused in the morning, Victoria feared they would peel the covers away to find their companion had passed in her sleep.

"Nothing that keeps you awake at night is silly, lass. The offer remains."

"I… didn't part from Mother and Father's care on good

terms," she confessed.

"And why is that?"

"Do you remember when I told you I turned down a marriage prospect? My parents told me I shamed them, Ramsay. Turning him down was unforgivable because it was a good match in their eyes."

"But not so good in yours?"

A bitter laugh escaped her when she thought back on their final argument, the words exchanged, and the overwhelming disappointment when they had failed to understand her desire to marry for love. She'd wanted what her cousin Anastasia had, so desperately it was worth leaving both her family and kingdom behind. "He once chased my cousin Anastasia and wanted to take her for his wife. I believe I was simply the second-best thing and as close as he could get to her, if that makes sense. He began to court me shortly after Uncle Morgan decided to marry Anastasia to the prince of Dalborough."

Ramsay snorted. "Foul place, Dalborough."

"Agreed."

"And this suitor? Where was he from?"

"Does it matter?" she asked.

"No, I suppose it doesn't. But tell me this, why did you turn him away?"

"Because I didn't love him."

"Love doesn't come all at once, lass. Did it not take several months for your cousin and King Alistair to fall in love?"

"I know that," she snapped. Her voice softened to a softer

 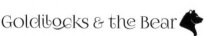

tone when she continued. "I didn't *want* to marry him. I didn't want to go become a queen in another kingdom. It would be like exchanging one cage for another. Before Anastasia married Alistair, I thought her to be so very lucky, but then I saw what they had and I yearned for the same thing."

"So you came to Cairn Ocland."

Her body relaxed beneath his touch as he ran his hand up and down her back in soothing strokes. "Yes. Ana saved me. She offered me the chance at freedom, and I took it. But…"

Ramsay waited, as patient as ever.

"But I still hid," she admitted. "I stayed in her castle and it took me a long while to realize it. Then, after the black fairy captured me, I realized I didn't ever want to be so weak and helpless again. I wanted to explore. To truly make Cairn Ocland my home."

"I imagine the wolves taught and showed you much."

The tight band constricting her chest eased. "They did. I learned all about the forests, how to track and hunt, and how to defend myself. But as much as I loved them all, I still didn't feel like it was the place I was meant to be. So I went back to Benthwaite. There I waited for a while until I decided it was time to come home and face my past."

"Do you still believe you need your parents to see the woman you've become?"

She rolled onto her back and looked up at him. "What do you mean?"

"That's why you're going home, isn't it?"

Ramsay settled down beside her again, only this time he tugged her close and wrapped his arms around her. She snuggled into his warmth, too cold and tired to resist.

Content to rest her cheek against his chest and hear the placid thump of his heart, Victoria closed her eyes and nuzzled close. Ramsay provided the ideal cushion, more perfect than any pillow. "You're right. I suppose part of why I'm doing this is to prove to them that I'm not a scared girl in need of their approval anymore."

"You're not. You're a fierce assassin of trolls and highwaymen," he teased. "But most importantly, you're my friend, and you're worth more than two of any spoiled noblemen. You know how to pull your own weight during a journey, you don't whine, and you're good at sneaking compliments out of an old grizzly bear."

"Oh, I don't know about that." Victoria ducked her face to hide her warm cheeks. "I've complained plenty."

"But never when it wasn't warranted. It's fine to complain, lass. Especially when you carry on with your head high. You aren't a quitter."

"No. I'm not, but I've wanted to."

Ramsay's lips grazed her temple. "Who cares of wanting? Actions are what matters most, and when it comes down to it, you've never let me down. Never forget that."

"I won't."

After overcoming her blushing cheeks, Victoria tilted her face up and studied Ramsay's features. The moonlight cast a silver glow on his face, highlighting his straight nose and full lips.

"Ramsay?"

"Hmm?" He didn't open his eyes.

Peeking toward Safiyya to make sure the old woman hadn't stirred, Victoria lowered her voice even further. "That first night in the cave… why did you—I mean, why haven't you done it again?"

His arms tightened around her. "I thought it was best to wait and speak to your father first."

"What?" Her brows drew together. "My father? What does that have to do with my father?"

"I wanted to tell him my intentions and receive his blessing for your hand." His eyes opened and he met her astonished gaze. "Isn't that what your people do?"

"It is," she whispered.

"Would you be opposed to my courting you?"

Despite the security of his embrace, she trembled against his chest, startled mute. "No," she whispered after a long silence.

Ramsay's lips turned up in a smile and he closed his eyes again. "Good. Now get some sleep. We have a long ride ahead of us."

Sleep? How did he expect her to sleep? Excitement made her heart beat faster. Ramsay wanted to court her. And for once, she wasn't opposed to, or agitated by the idea. Settling her head back down against his shoulder, she closed her eyes and willed her racing pulse to slow.

Patience, she told herself. All she needed was patience, and sooner or later, their affection would take care of the rest.

Chapter 12

THEY PRESSED ON by stopping only when necessary to rest the horses and stretch their legs. The promise of a town with a proper inn was all the motivation any of them needed. Throughout their ride to Dunville, Victoria noticed Safiyya appeared more exhausted by the second, but the old woman remained too stubborn to take a break.

As they crested the hill, she saw their destination in the distance, aglow in warm orange colors beneath the setting sun. "There! In the distance! I can see the town. Dunville is our greatest city next to Lorehaven," Victoria explained. "My family and I lived here for a time until Uncle Morgan gifted us with a beautiful home in the city."

Afterward, there hadn't been any visits to the north because she'd lived within a five-minute ride of the castle and could see her cousin whenever she desired.

Victoria smiled at the memory and led the group toward a friendly inn known across northern Creag Morden for its soft beds, delicious hotcakes, and savory dinner rolls. Given the opportunity to have a room of her own, she forked over the coins necessary, despite the significant mark-up. She'd never heard such outrageous prices before, but the nervous innkeeper insisted the prices were always high.

It didn't stop her from paying an additional coin for a tub and hot water to be taken to her room posthaste. The others did the same, each of them ready for a night of comfort and privacy. By the time they had enjoyed their fine meal of lamb, roasted vegetables, and buttered rolls, the bartender approached the table to inform them that their baths were ready.

She paid the bill and left a more generous payment than what she thought he deserved before they retired to the tavern's upper level.

"I'll see the two of you in the morning then. Good night, Safiyya. Sleep well, Ramsay."

"G'night, lass. Sleep tight." He lingered in his doorway, watching her.

"Sleep well, lovely," Safiyya said in her gentle, grandmotherly voice.

Victoria shut the door behind her and turned the latch, grateful for a night of peace, privacy, and quiet. Ramsay snored louder than a rusty minecart, and Safiyya talked in her sleep. It was a peculiar thing, as the woman always seemed to be pleading for someone's forgiveness, and the name certainly didn't sound like Samiran to her. Had it been Rumpelstiltskin?

Despite her curiosity, Victoria couldn't bring herself to pry and ask, even if she had stayed awake an hour past stretching out beside the sorceress in bed.

Free of anyone to share her room, she closed the window

shutters, turned up the oil lantern, and eyed the still-steaming bath.

"At last," she murmured.

While a quick dip in a stream along the way had washed the worst of the grime and dust from her gnomish adventure away, she had still felt filthy. Victoria took a generous handful of scented salts from the selection provided and stirred them into the hot water. A sweet floral fragrance drifted up on the curling steam, and she happily slid in, releasing a blissful sigh.

She soaked her aches away first then applied soap to her body and hair with a hard scrubbing. Only after she'd scoured her skin pink and rid every nail of embedded dirt did she crawl from the water and into a thick robe. When she unplugged the drain, water ran out a small pipe and was carried away outside the room to the world below.

Plumbing, a new technology to finally reach Creag Morden, had taken all the villages by storm and there was no shortage of young men desperate to learn the trade. Of course, such things had already prospered in Cairn Ocland, and some of their best masters had traveled abroad to teach it.

Victoria smiled. It was nice to see the kingdoms sharing knowledge, trading, and working together. Anastasia had thrown all her love and effort into uniting both nations.

But what can I do, she wondered. An oval mirror hung on the wall opposite her, large enough to reflect her features from the shoulders up. She saw tired eyes, damp hair, porcelain skin, and rosy cheeks still reddened from the bath. She was no famed huntress capable of taking down a grand fairy. No great sorceress with the power to defeat an army.

Victoria studied her face, her lean arms, and her slender body, while comparing herself to all the great women in her life. *Who am I? I'm no one,* replied the niggling voice of doubt residing in her deepest, darkest worries. *I can barely hold my own against huntresses trained their entire lives to fight. I'll never be strong like Sorcha or wise as Ana.*

No, the tiny voice of her self-confidence disagreed. *You are Lady Victoria, slayer of trolls. You helped an old woman to cross a kingdom, discovered a forgotten nation, and before this week ends, you will reunite two lovers who have waited centuries to find one another again. You are someone, whether Lord and Lady Summersfield recognize it or not.*

Growing prouder by the second, Victoria smiled. "I can't wait to tell Anastasia." There were so many stories to share, though she longed to chat about her adventures sooner. Tempted, she set out the small bowl carved from a lightning-struck oak that Ana had attuned to her crystal ball, and then she filled it with water. "Just in case."

By the time she combed out her hair until the golden strands shone, she felt like a new woman.

"Victoria?"

Her cousin's voice came from the bowl she'd set on the bedside table. Victoria hurried over and looked down into the glowing water.

"I thought you might be checking up on me soon," she

said, smiling at Ana's image.

"Am I so predictable?"

Victoria laughed. Seeing her cousin's face, hearing her voice, brought a deep sense of comfort. She'd missed her. "I know you, cousin, that's all. Besides, I'd *hoped* you'd call, which is why I set up the bowl."

"Where are you? That doesn't look like the bedroom I remember. Did your parents change your room?"

"I'm not in Lorehaven. Not yet anyway."

"What?" Ana's eyes widened and she looked away, checking something beyond sight of her crystal ball. "Why are you in Dunville? You should be home by now."

"It's a bit of a story. Suffice to say, a storm held me up once I passed through the mountains and now I'm traveling with someone."

"Oh? Do tell."

"There's not much to tell," Victoria fibbed. "A few roadside bandits, storms, and price-gouging merchants. My friend and I met along the way." Part of her worried Ana would swoop in, full of motherly concern, if she told her everything that had happened. As much as she loved her cousin, she didn't want to be rescued. "He's most likely asleep by now or I'd introduce you."

The image of Anastasia shifted in the reflective water surface. "You're traveling with a man?"

Victoria's cheeks warmed. "As a friend."

"Ah, so that's why you're redder than a bottle of blush

wine. Because of your *friend*."

The heat didn't fade. Victoria ducked her face and cupped her palms against her cheeks. "It's nothing of the sort, I mean… it's… it's complicated."

"Aren't all relationships complicated? If things were simple, there'd be no excitement." Anastasia gestured with one hand toward someone out of the frame created by the water bowl. "I'll be up soon."

"Who's that?" Alistair called in the distance.

"It's Victoria. I finally caught her in my crystal ball."

"Ah. Tell her I said hello then. Glad to know she's doing well."

"Alistair says hello, and now he's gone off to bed like the old man he is." A big smile spread over Anastasia's face. Her husband wasn't yet forty, and certainly didn't appear to be reaching middle age. "There, now we're alone to talk girlish things."

"There's not much to say. I poured a bowl of water when I realized you might be inclined to check in on my progress."

"How about starting with why you aren't in Lorehaven? Are you simply taking your time to enjoy the company?"

"If you must know, I'm enjoying an adventure," Victoria straightened her spine. "Did you know there was a gnomish city beneath Creag Morden?"

Ana's eyes widened. "What? Truly?"

There was a certain sense of smug satisfaction that swept over her upon discovering she knew something her brilliant cousin didn't. "Yes. Ramsay and I explored it in depth. We even ran into trolls."

She recounted the underground adventure, leaving out nothing except her one selfish moment with Ramsay. That memory was hers and hers alone.

"Oh my, you really *are* having an adventure. It almost makes me wish I had come along," Ana said. "So what's next?"

"We're headed for Lorehaven. I hate to admit it, but I'll be glad for a comfortable bed."

"And some privacy?" Ana prompted. "Really, Victoria, days alone with a handsome man and you feel nothing? Not even a little interest?"

"I…" She knit her fingers into the edge of one sleeve.

Ana's brows drew inward and her forehead wrinkled. "Vicky, love, you know you can talk to me about anything."

"When we were alone in the gnomish undercity, he touched me." After a breath or two in and out of her lungs to steel herself, she added in a low voice, "Quite intimately."

Ana's smile gradually diminished, and her mouth pressed into a thin line. "Was it against your will? If he—"

"No. It wasn't anything like that."

The hard lines of her cousin's face softened with relief. "Good."

"I liked it, Ana. And he was gentle. But all he did was touch, and he hasn't again since." Victoria bit her lower lip. "He wants to ask Mother and Father for my hand the official way as humans do in Creag Morden. But first, he asked me if it would make me happy."

"That's certainly a point in his favor. And how do you feel about it?"

"I said yes. How couldn't I? I'm long past marrying age… almost eight years in Cairn Ocland, and I still haven't found a husband."

"To be honest, I always wondered why you never settled down. But I decided it wasn't any of my business," Anastasia admitted. "You were happy, and that mattered most to me. Without Uncle Humphrey troubling you over shaming the family or my own father attempting to find you noble marriage prospects, I thought you would determine your future in your own time."

"Thank you for that."

"There's no need to thank me for doing what's right, cousin. After all, there is nothing of greater importance than your personal satisfaction in a match. But I did wish I could give you a fraction of the profound pleasure I've found while being Alistair's wife."

"I wouldn't have minded if you'd said anything, Ana. You rescued me from Mother and Father's obstinacy. You brought me to a home where I can be myself."

"I also put you in great danger."

"When?"

Anastasia straightened her back and glanced away, but moisture shone in her eyes. "It's nothing."

"No, it's certainly something. Did you forget how well I

 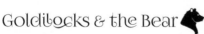

know you, cousin? That you can speak to *me* too, of anything?" Victoria pressed in a soft-spoken voice.

After a moment of silence, Anastasia tucked her chin. "It's silly, but...when Maeval abducted you, I... felt... I've always felt as if I failed you that day."

"*No.*" The word left her in a hard, unyielding utterance. "You won't blame yourself for that. The only one to blame is Maeval... and perhaps a little of the blame is mine for my weakness. When I came to your home, I had the opportunity to learn to fight. I could have asked any number of guards to teach me. But instead, I did nothing. I depended on others to be my defense. I let guardsmen be my shield."

"And now you're standing on your own against bandits and escaping trolls in gnomish undercities." Anastasia blinked away a few tears. "I'm quite proud of you, cousin. Still, is there anything Alistair or I may do to help? Should I send aid to patrol the roads? Should we come ourselves to breathe fire and instill fear in their treacherous little hearts?"

"No. They're only thieves. Promise to come only if you want to visit your family."

Anastasia chuckled. "I visited Mother and Father a month ago, so I'm not due for some time. Now, tell me of your travel companion. You spoke of your adventure with him, but tell me of the man himself. Who is he?"

The heat resurfaced, making Victoria want to hide her face within her nightshift collar. "His name is Ramsay of Clan Ardal."

Her cousin's mouth fell open. "*That* Ramsay. *Father Bear?* You've traveled all this time with a clan leader?"

"I know it's unseemly, but he's a good man."

"I know he is. I've met him before and adore all the leaders of Clan Ardal equally. Especially Mother Bear. She's an amazing woman, and I doubt she'd speak so highly of Ramsay if he wasn't fit to lead beside her." Anastasia clasped her hands together. "I'm so happy for you."

"Happy for what? We're not yet truly betrothed until Father agrees—"

"Victoria, you're thirty years old. If ever there is a time to do what you want, it's now. Who gives a damn what Uncle Humphrey thinks. Will they know?"

"Well, no… I suppose not."

"What you and Ramsay choose to do in private is for you to decide alone. Do you want a large Mordenian wedding?"

Victoria couldn't imagine enduring the five-hour long ceremony before the entire city in Lorehaven's enormous cathedral anymore than she could picture forcing Ramsay to uphold their beliefs. Weddings in Cairn Ocland varied significantly, as they were nonexistent, no more than a private vow between mates. If any celebration did occur in public, it was a feast the following day and blessings to the new couple.

When she didn't answer, Ana continued. "Do you care whether or not Ramsay has your parents' permission?"

"No. No, I don't. They don't run my life."

"Then take charge and do what makes you happy, dear

 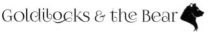

cousin."

"Thanks, Ana. I suppose I needed to hear it from someone else."

"Sometimes that's all we need," her wise cousin said. "Enjoy the rest of your time back home. Love you."

"Love you too."

"Also… the first time doesn't hurt. Not the way the romance novels from Creag Morden claim it does, anyway."

"*What?*"

As heat surged to Victoria's face, Ana's image faded away, leaving only the flickering glow of candlelight reflecting off the water. Victoria dumped the bowl and thought about everything they'd talked about. Ana was right. It was her life, and only she had a say in what she did with it. Not her parents.

And right now, she wanted nothing more than to claim her man.

After fetching her lockpicks and her room key from the table, she blew out the bedside candle, stepped outside, and secured the door. All abuzz with anticipation, Victoria crouched in the quiet hallway with her pickset and finagled the metal blades into Ramsay's lock. It took only a few seconds to pop the three tumblers, and then the door crept inward.

Was the lock merely easy, or had she become that good? The question lingered in the back of her mind as she proceeded into Ramsay's room and shut the door behind her. She locked it back and set her room key and picks on the table with a dull thud, half hoping the noise would awaken him.

VIVIENNE SAVAGE

It didn't. He lay in bed, unstirring and still, an enormous mountain of a man in only his smallclothes, without a blanket. He'd kicked that and the linen sheets toward the foot of the bed, leaving his entire body exposed. Victoria flushed.

"Ramsay," she whispered.

When he didn't arouse to the sound of her voice, she trailed her fingers over his chest through the caramel brown hair only a few shades darker than his blond curls. As a bear, he'd been beautiful, but he took her breath away in his human body.

Now or never. I've made up my mind.

After a brief internal debate, Victoria removed her shift and crawled into bed beside him, positive her racing heart would awaken him first. Ramsay proved to be dead to the world instead, his noisy rumbles quieting to a grouchy mumble in his sleep.

"Vic... Victoria."

"Yes?" she whispered back.

He quieted again, leaving her on the proverbial edge of her seat until she realized he'd only spoken her name in his sleep. Did he dream of her? The thought made her giddy and all the more certain about her path. She thought of what Anastasia had said, then took charge.

Kissing Ramsay was every bit as empowering as she'd hoped it would be. He startled awake, impossibly still until he came to his senses and trailed one broad palm down her naked back. He cupped one bare cheek and squeezed while making a delightful, bearlike rumble in his chest.

"I'm not dreaming."

She stole another playful kiss. "No."

"You're not wearing anything."

"Not a stitch," she confirmed. Her body tingled while she awaited his answer. When he didn't respond, feeling with one hand below his waist gave her all the reaction she needed.

He growled low in his throat and rolled her beneath him, leaning back on his knees to study her body in its entirety. The pale shafts of moonlight spilling through the adjacent window made his torso a masterpiece of highlighted planes and shadowed valleys. Her eyes followed every muscular curve, and then she stroked her fingers through the soft curls on his chest. It was her favorite part of him.

"What are you doing, Goldi?"

"Taking charge."

Although she didn't know the first thing about what she was doing, she slipped her fingers between his skin and the close-fitting linen he wore, and then she tore it. It ripped easily, exposing him.

And every glorious inch became hers to touch. A combination of cool air and excitement covered her skin in goose bumps, while Ramsay eyed her through half-lidded bedroom eyes. He rose tall and proud, hard as polished marble in her hands, but far more responsive than any statue.

"Never wear trousers or smallclothes again."

"Why not?" he asked in a husky growl.

How could she possibly tell him how much she preferred his kilt, and how she'd grown accustomed to the green and silver garment fluttering around his knees and thighs? For fear of bloating his ego, she didn't utter a word regarding how often she'd prayed to the wind, hoping it would toss the blasted thing around his waist. Heat rushed to her face as her gaze traveled over his chiseled body from abdomen to chest. She traced the same path with her fingers and gave in to the urge to explore.

He mimicked her and slid his hand over her ribs until he reached her right breast. The nipple tightened beneath his thumb. "Too shy to answer, are you?"

"No, I…" She blinked a few times before her gaze darted to the lantern on the bedside table. It was a pity she hadn't invaded his room earlier to make love by lantern light. "I want to admire you," she admitted in a tiny voice. "You're perfect and beautiful."

If she hadn't already confirmed stonecraft to be his only gift, she would have thought he'd read her mind too. He reached beside them with one hand and clicked the striker on the oil lantern, igniting a small flame.

"I won't make love to you in the dark, lass."

Before she could respond, he bowed his head over her. Sparks of ecstasy lit across her skin when his mouth descended to her breasts, and then he kissed each firm swell while introducing his tongue to the rosy tips. She arched beneath him, struck dumb by his mouth before her mind could articulate an elegant compliment befitting her noble bear.

"Ramsay…"

He released one nipple with a gentle pop. "I assume you know what this means now, for us to meet here in bed after our last discussion in camp."

"That we'll be joined according to your customs. Wed and bonded."

"Aye." He separated her thighs, resting one on each side of his hips. At first, she thought it was to admire or even claim her as his mate, and then his devious intentions came to light when his thumb touched her center and circled over the sensitive sweet spot. While guarding her virginity like a precious gift for so many years, she'd only tentatively explored her body in absolute privacy.

"If lovemaking leads to marriage for your kind… how does…? No, never mind." She didn't want to think of him with other women, whether they were shifter or human.

His husky chuckle warmed her throat. "How have I gone all my life without making love to a woman? It depends on what you consider a virgin, lass. The word doesn't exist in the Oclander tongue, not in the way your countrymen would use it."

Another flick of his thumb teased her. Victoria's thoughts dissolved into a haze of bliss with each pass.

"What… what word is it then?" When the first of his thick digits entered her, it became a struggle to utter intelligent words.

"*Gangrannach.* It's the word we use for one who isn't yet

loved by their other half. Whether shifter or human, we wait for as long as we're able. No one before you exists in my mind or memories anymore, because this… this I've been saving for you alone."

She trembled beneath him and pressed her toes against the sheets, the shifting fabric a whisper of sound quieter than her drumming heartbeat.

"But you didn't even know me."

"I knew you existed out there, somewhere, and that was good enough. Now that I've answered your questions, you answer one of mine. Were we not to wait and ask your mum and da'?"

"Well… I spoke with Ana and realized what was most important to *me*," she replied, with renewed courage surging through her veins. "I don't want a large wedding in a temple. I want you, my *friend,* and the one man to ever care what *I* want. I've never been more certain about anything."

Ramsay had chosen the perfect position in bed, kneeling between Victoria's legs with the blankets piled behind him. The twin indents on either side of his hips carved a perfect arrow to the arousal jutting toward his navel. After curling her fingers around him, she guided the bear's length to the pulsing ache between her thighs. Ramsay pulled her hand away and raised her fingers to his lips, holding her gaze as he surged forward to claim her one stroke at a time.

Her body resisted him, the grip tighter than she'd anticipated, but when he faltered and gave her time to adjust to his size, she hooked her ankle behind his buttocks and dragged him forward.

The next thrust introduced her to a fleeting twinge of discomfort, but the pleasure of their union snuffed the pain as quickly as a candle flame. Ramsay kissed her fingers again and held still, his body poised tight above hers while he waited.

"You're beautiful," he whispered against her palm, laying a trail of kisses up to her wrist. "Beautiful and perfect."

Ramsay's patience and tender touches gave her the time she needed to adjust. He watched her, his golden-brown eyes never leaving her face, and when the tension eased from her body, he made his first backstroke. Victoria gasped and grabbed his shoulder with one hand, the other on his back.

"Do you like that, lass?"

"Yes. Do it again."

His laughter feathered across her throat as he leaned down, but he met her request and joined their bodies anew. Victoria closed her eyes and followed his lead, letting her own desires guide her as much as Ramsay's gentle touch. She learned his rhythm and met it, then challenged him for more by speeding up her pace.

Tender, sweet, and slow became urgent and frenzied. They rolled across the mattress without care for the sheets and pillows, and then Ramsay lifted her from the blankets, pulling her atop his lap as he sat up.

"Mine." His voice rumbled deep in his chest. He cupped one breast in his large hand and pushed it upward to meet his descending mouth. The tingle fluttered all the way from the rosy peak to her core and clenched around him.

"Yours," she whispered. She ran her fingers down his arms and back up again, delighting in the way his muscles bunched and flexed beneath her touch.

Her Ramsay. Hers. Hers to explore and touch. Hers to kiss with all the desire she could muster. And hers to love, even though she couldn't yet force the words from her lips.

With his hands guiding her hips, they moved together in a wild tempo matched only by their beating hearts. Tension coiled within her limbs, a strange pressure building further and further, until she felt ready to explode.

"Ramsay," she gasped. Her fingers clutched his shoulder and back.

Her voice pitched higher until she called his name out in a joyous cry. An unquenchable fire raged inside her, pleasure burning through every limb. Ramsay moaned in turn and her entire world shifted, though their bodies never stopped, hips grinding together in a delicious churn.

Victoria spiraled into ecstasy, riding through one sensation after the next while her emotions soared to impossible heights. They reached the plateau together, achieving a surreal moment when she felt his heart and hers beating as one.

"Ramsay!"

He buried his face against her hair and the cool pillow cradling her head. Mutual release initiated a chain of sensation, a storm of pleasure building anew and reaching a dramatic crescendo. He didn't stop, her tireless and inexhaustible lover, until at last she shuddered again and they were both spent.

It took as much time to catch her breath as it had to enjoy the act itself. Amused by that realization, she shifted beneath his solid bulk and savored the skin-on-skin contact.

"My bear," she panted when she regained some control over her lungs. "Mine."

"Yours always." He rolled, pulling her with him so the heated connection between their bodies never broke. Once he was on his back with her sprawled atop his chest, he hugged her close, one hand cupping her bottom and the other splayed between her shoulder blades.

"Will it always be like this?" she asked.

His warm chuckle stirred her hair, and the sweet sound of it made her tingle from head to toe. "This and better. We have all our lives to learn how to please one another."

"I like the sound of that." She smiled.

"Get some sleep while you can, lass. I don't intend to let you have much."

"What?" Her voice squeaked, and Ramsay laughed again, squeezing her bottom.

"I'll never tire of doing that. You have no idea how long I've wanted to."

"I could guess…" Her mind went back to his kilt and those delectable peeks of firm thigh whenever the wind disturbed it.

He stroked her back, skimming his fingers up and down her spine until her breaths evened out and her eyelids drifted shut. In Ramsay, she'd found a man who understood her, who respected her as much as she respected him. A man who stirred the fire in her heart, both anger and passion, but could also bring her a sweet comfort and sympathetic ear.

She couldn't ask for a better man to take as a husband.

"Goodnight, my husband," she said in a quiet voice, relishing the word. She'd really done it, taking an unbreakable physical and verbal vow of matrimony.

"Goodnight, my wife," he whispered against her hair. "My Goldilocks."

Until she'd experienced the joy of lying in Ramsay's arms, Victoria had never felt safer, and the promise of them belonging to her forever was all the comfort she needed as she drifted to sleep.

Chapter 13

RAMSAY AWAKENED FIRST to find yellow hair fanned over his bare chest. The sun shone bright over the thin linen sheets and turned each individual strand into a thread of spun gold. After a night filled with more activity than sleep, he felt justified in their late awakening.

He considered sliding out from beneath her to dress and acquire food, but he couldn't bear to move and risk awakening her. After weighing the risk against the reward, he crept out of bed gently enough to leave her undisturbed.

The stars had blessed him. He'd known it from the moment he asked permission to court her beneath the velvet sky, when he'd pleaded with them to have finally given him the special mate meant to be his wife and his alone. After using the shallow wash basin for a brief scrub, he tossed on his tunic and his kilt then hurried down the steps with hopes of returning before Victoria awakened.

Safiyya awaited him at the bar, her crooked spine bent over a cup of steaming tea. "It's about time you roused, Ramsay, although I must say I thought you'd sleep in as late as Victoria."

"Uh."

She fixed him with a knowing look and chuckled. "I may

be old, but my memories of being in love are intact. I took the liberty of ordering for you. Ah, here it comes now."

A servant carried out a tray loaded with fried eggs, thick slices of bacon, hot cakes, and fresh berries. A pot of tea sat in the center of it all, two cups stacked to the side with the silverware.

"Thank you… um." He cleared his throat and looked to the servant. "The lady will require another hot bath in her room."

"Of course, sir. Right away."

"Go on, shoo." A smile brightened Safiyya's wrinkled face and deepened the creases at the corners of her mouth. The brown spots on the back of her hand had darkened, and what little color she'd had in her hair was fading. Each day, she aged a little more in front of them. "Take all of the time you desire. I'll be here once you're both ready."

"Thank you, Safiyya."

He returned upstairs with breakfast for two to find Victoria awake and waiting for him, sprawled upon her belly.

"I'd hoped to surprise you," Ramsay admitted as he set the tray on a small table beneath the window.

"You did."

"Are you hungry?"

"I am, though not for food at the moment." She leaned up on her elbows and crooked a finger at him.

She didn't need to say anything more. He abandoned their meal and rejoined her in the bed, happy to let his wife push him to his back and claim him from above.

At last, he'd met his match and found a woman who didn't literally send him fleeing to the hills. While Victoria wasn't a bear, she was the embodiment of everything else he'd desired in a mate. There was no one better suited for him, and he'd long decided her tenacity in the face of danger only made her braver than his powerful clan sisters.

Victoria had been made for him, a gift from the stars, and he'd never regret a day of heeding Heldreth and Talbot's advice. Visiting Creag Morden hadn't merely granted him a reprieve from his duties: a holiday in her kingdom had brought him to the love of his life.

And nothing would ever make him take her for granted.

Enough distance spanned between Dunville and Lorehaven for Victoria to realize they wouldn't arrive until long after dark, so with Ramsay's aid, she managed to convince Safiyya to take a night of rest before facing Aladdin on the morrow.

"Look, I see Bellbrook!" Victoria's spirit's soared higher as the village came into view on the horizon. As the last little town before reaching the royal capital, Bellbrook saw frequent traffic from Lorehaven and had grown prosperous over the years without expanding in population.

It didn't take long for her enthusiasm to dim. As they turned onto the narrow road leading to town, they were passed by an exodus of people traveling on the western road

VIVIENNE SAVAGE

toward Dalborough. Villagers scurried around them, giving a wide berth while avoiding eye contact.

"Excuse me," Victoria called to a passing merchant. His gaze darted up to her in acknowledgment before he tried to move past them. Ramsay blocked his path.

"The lady addressed you," the bear said in a disapproving voice, a deep frown on his face. "Surely you can spare her a moment?"

"What do you want?" the man said. "Please, I must go with what little I have left."

"What do you mean?" Victoria asked. "Has something happened in Bellbrook? Sickness?"

The merchant licked his lips and darted his gaze back to the road, clearly in a rush to get away from them and the city. He hitched his pack up higher on his shoulders. The overstuffed canvas jingled as the items within shifted. "No plague, miss, but something far worse. At least a plague can be cured by a talented apothecary, but there's no medicine for this trouble."

"Then tell me, please," Victoria said in exasperation. She peered down from Rook's saddle at the merchant, unwilling to dismount while they were surrounded by chaos.

"There are bandits about and they'll be here soon, mark my words," the merchant told them.

"Bandits?"

"You mean bandits have the entire village on the run?" Ramsay asked.

"That's preposterous." Victoria blinked and furrowed her

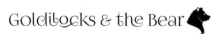

Goldilocks & the Bear

brow. "We'll go to Lorehaven and have them send out guards to secure the roads."

The merchant blanched and grabbed hold of Victoria's leg. Rook shuffled to the side, but the man's terrified grip didn't loosen. "No, miss, I beseech you. Lorehaven isn't a place you want to go right now. It's been taken over by the Forty Thieves, the most notorious gang of murderers to ever darken Creag Morden's soil."

"What do you mean taken over?" she whispered. "What about my uncle? Where is King Morgan? He wouldn't stand for such nonsense."

Paling further, the merchant released her and bowed until his long beard touched the ground and the weight of his belongings threw him off balance. Ramsay reached down and steadied him.

"My lady, forgive me, but word has it the king and queen have been thrown in the dungeon. It's said he plans to execute His Majesty tomorrow at sunset and perhaps even the queen as well. Few people escaped before the city was sealed off, but they all carry the same tale. Aladdin has proclaimed himself ruler of Lorehaven Castle, and it's only a matter of time before he sacks Bellbrook. His men already razed Windhollow to the east. Hundreds are dead for refusing to bend knee to him! Now, our only hope is to cross the borders to Dalborough."

"Please, sir, you must tell me of Lord and Lady Summersfield. Do you know anything else?" Were her parents locked away as well? What about the palace guards?

VIVIENNE SAVAGE

"Not much, my lady, no. They said he has claimed all the loveliest maidens in the land for his harem in lieu of a noble-born wife since the princess is gone and wed already. The governor released his fastest messenger bird to Queen Anastasia, but I fear—"

"It will be too late," Victoria finished for him in a quiet voice.

"Yes, my lady. Please, you must turn away. Get as far from here as you can."

With no one else blocking his way, the merchant continued to scurry down the road. Ramsay brought Dunn up beside Rook and reached over for Victoria's hand. She hated the way it trembled.

"We have to help," she said. Her gaze snapped over to Safiyya. "It was Samiran, wasn't it? That's how he's done this."

"Likely so, yes." Safiyya's tortured gaze lowered away in shame.

"No, don't blame yourself," Victoria hastily said. "I don't blame your husband. He's a slave, forced to do as he's told. But we have to fix this."

"I hadn't expected Aladdin to take control of an entire kingdom. That's a lofty goal, especially for a thief. I don't know how we can get to him now."

"We'll start by finding somewhere safe to figure it out," Ramsay said. "We cannot stay here. If that merchant is right, we don't want to be on the highway when he combs the area again. I suggest we make for the hills and set up camp

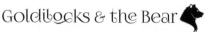
Goldilocks & the Bear

somewhere hidden."

Lacking a contrary argument against the suggestion, Victoria guided them off the road and into the thin woodlands to the west. None of them spoke, although she felt Ramsay's worried gaze on her more often than not.

Even as darkness fell, they continued onward with Ramsay in the lead. Having come to trust his sense for stone and earth, Victoria prayed it meant he could locate a suitable hiding ground.

"Here," Ramsay called out. "It's an old bear den. Empty for now."

Barely able to see in the dark, Victoria made out the silhouette of a rocky hill face in the deep shadows but little else until Safiyya summoned a small witchlight. The pale blue glow revealed a shallow but wide hollow in the hill.

Whether it was because of her magic use or the cooler weather, Safiyya shivered beside her. Victoria embraced her friend and rubbed the old woman's arms. "Can we risk a small fire, do you think?" she asked. With darkness upon them and the cool autumn night laying blankets of shadow across the land, the occasional wind gust twisted beneath their shelter and through the den.

"Aye," Ramsay replied. "You two sit. I'll fetch some wood. It's safe enough with the rock hiding the light."

While he went off in search of kindling, Victoria and Safiyya huddled together for warmth, although the latter shivered long after he returned and started the fire. Fear made

VIVIENNE SAVAGE

Victoria quiet, despair and her healthy imagination dreaming up a thousand devilish crimes committed against her family by the thieves.

"Now what are we to do?" Ramsay broke the silence at last when no one else would speak up. "There's no telling what monstrosities Aladdin has had your ifrit conjure up to do his bidding," he said while tending the flames.

"That's what worries me," Victoria replied. "We can't quit now."

Safiyya sighed. "She's right. This is my last chance to free Samiran. I refuse to die without trying."

"Forgive me, Safiyya, but that's what concerns me. I fear you wouldn't survive any sort of battle." Ramsay ran both hands through his blond curls, appearing divided.

"I won't ask you two to accompany me. You have done enough by risking your lives for the ring and the hammer. I cannot ask for more, and I won't endanger you further to do an errand I ought to have completed years ago. If I'd only opened my eyes… If I'd looked beyond my heartbreak and realized Samiran needed me, Aladdin wouldn't have him now. All of this is my fault."

"It is *not*," Victoria disagreed. "If ifrit are truly such capricious creatures, why were you to believe anything else?"

Moisture glistened in Safiyya's misty eyes. "I should have believed in his love for me," she spoke in a low, monotone voice. "But I allowed his sister's spite to damage my trust in him. She told me he would forget me one day… and like a fool,

I listened. I can't ask for you to risk your life while righting my wrong."

"You don't have to," Victoria said before Ramsay could disagree. "I want to help you. Besides, Aladdin has made this personal now. Lorehaven was my home."

"What of your cousin?" Safiyya asked. "That man said they sent word."

Ramsay shook his head. "We can't be sure she'll receive the message. That's a long trip for a bird, which means it won't arrive for days. Though…" He cut his gaze toward Victoria. "You said you spoke with her. How?"

"A scrying bowl, but I can't initiate the contact and, well, I told her not to check on me for a few days because I was with you. She'll honor that request, so that's not an option."

Her husband swore under his breath. "That puts us at a distinct disadvantage. It would be dangerous even with a dragon alongside us, but nigh impossible alone, the three of us and a single jinni."

"I'm going, Ramsay. With or without you. That's my family."

"I'm not saying we give up, lass, only that it'd be unwise to attempt retaking the city now. Your uncle wouldn't want you to die in vain."

Blinking back her tears, she stared at him and wondered if he was right, if she was thinking with her emotion instead of her sense. And if it mattered whether she was. Were it not for Anastasia and the king's adamant belief that she should go to

Cairn Ocland to seek a new life, she'd still be in the city, a sad spinster, or perhaps forcefully married to Prince Joren.

Expecting a standoff between them, or even a longer argument, Victoria held her breath.

The knotted tension in Ramsay's shoulders loosened and the hard lines of his face softened. In a gentler voice, he murmured, "Safiyya, what needs to be done to free Samiran?"

Victoria sagged in relief. "Thank you," she whispered to him.

"The only way to end this siege against Creag Morden is for one of you to get me the lamp. Nothing has changed. With the enchanted hammer, I'll obliterate the binding runes on the lamp."

"Easy as that?" he asked.

"Yes."

"I know how we can get in the city unseen," Victoria said. Both Ramsay and Safiyya turned their eyes on her. "There are two entrances via a secret passage."

"You know how to enter?" Ramsay asked.

Victoria nodded. "Uncle Morgan showed Ana and me every inch of it shortly after Alistair first began to attack the kingdom. He and Sir Williford walked us through the entire route and showed us how to operate the doors."

Safiyya inclined her head in silent approval. "So we have a way inside. Into the palace, I assume?"

"Yes," Victoria replied. "There are two entries through the same passage. One is in the throne room and the other in the scullery."

"Good. Now how do we get the lamp from Aladdin?" Ramsay crossed his arms over his chest. "Sounds like something he'd keep close by."

"We'll cross that bridge when we come to it," Victoria replied. "For now, we should get moving."

"No, first we are going to rest." Ramsay covered her mouth before she could speak against him and continued. "We'll save no one, Victoria, if we're falling over tired. We rode long and hard today hoping to get to the town, so for now we are going to rest. A few hours at the very least. Maziar can keep watch for us."

"Fine," she agreed, though everything in her screamed to get moving. Despite her own impatience, she recognized that a few hours would benefit everyone, especially to mount a rescue against a madman with access to an all-powerful fire elemental's magic.

Chapter 14

VICTORIA FOUND THE entrance to the underground catacombs in the western woods not far from a stone circle where the followers of Creag Morden's old religion once prayed to the gods of the earth.

Although it was locked from the inside, Victoria twisted a small stone nearby and the rocky slab concealing the passage rolled into the ground to grant them admittance. Once they descended into the earth, she depressed an emblem in the wall and closed the entrance behind them. Ever-burning torches, an enchantment that created continuous fire without consuming the source, crackled on either side of the corridor.

"Ana and I used to sneak into these tunnels to play when we were young. Her father was livid when he found out and mine was scandalized. This is no place for a lady, after all." She raised a torch from its holder and shone it over the faded murals covering the stone walls. "While we've always known of the tunnels, we never knew there was a way to exit the city through them. In hindsight, Father and Uncle Morgan's fury makes sense to me. Imagine if we've gotten out and lost in the wilderness."

Ramsay chuckled quietly behind them and squeezed her

shoulder. "Another adventure for you and your cousin."

"Is this another gnomish city beneath the ground?" Safiyya asked.

"No. These crypts were built by our ancestors," Victoria explained. "Some call this the city of the dead. The entire royal family is interred down here."

"Perhaps now would be a wise time to make a plan," Ramsay suggested. "Before we go any farther and risk discovery."

"Right." Victoria set the torch in a holder on the wall. "Well, the tunnel is simple enough. There are no twists or turns we need to take. If we follow this main path, it will lead directly to both entrances. If you veer into the side passages, it's easy to get lost."

"Where does the tunnel lead out?"

"The first entrance lets out in the throne room. It's marked with an eagle medallion set in the wall. You simply tug the left wing down and the wall opens."

"The throne room is undoubtedly guarded," Ramsay muttered.

"Yes, I imagine so," Victoria said. "But you can use the spyhole to look at least."

"And the second?" Safiyya asked.

"Lets out in the larder at the back of the palace. That's the closest entrance to the dungeons as well. But you'll have to make it through the kitchens first. There's a ladder at the end of the tunnel we'll have to climb, but it's short. The trapdoor is always covered by an old rug and usually a few bags of flour or corn. If you take the tunnel past the ladder, it eventually leads out on the eastern side of the city into an old graveyard."

"All right. So we use the larder entrance and make our way to the lower levels," Ramsay said. "We can then lead the king and queen back to the tunnel."

"But what about Aladdin?" Victoria crossed her arms over her chest. "He needs to be distracted so he doesn't realize we're making off with his prisoners."

"What about Maziar? Can't he be of use?" Ramsay looked pointedly at the ring on Safiyya's finger.

"A jinni is no match for an ifrit, unfortunately," Safiyya said. "If he's ordered, Samiran will have no choice but to hurt us or do whatever he must at Aladdin's behest. He has no control. He's a puppet. The one advantage we have is that Samiran is unable to take human lives unprovoked, or force us to behave against our wills, but there's a great deal more a creative mind can demand if he wants to cause pain."

Victoria raked her fingers through her hair and sat on one of the low crypts. "Then we can't use a wish to help us here. Not if we want to hide our possession of Maziar."

"I don't know," the older woman admitted. "I am hopeful an opportunity will present itself."

An opportunity. No matter how Victoria considered their options, it practically spelled doom.

Sorrow deflated what remained of her hopes when she thought of the poor girls stolen from their homes, the people robbed in broad daylight, and the slain guards unable to defend them.

"What if… what if an unmarried noblewoman approached him and was able to wrest the lamp from his possession?" Victoria asked. "What would happen then? He can't keep the lamp in his possession at all times, can he?"

"Absolutely not." Ramsay straightened and drew himself up to his full height. Victoria wasn't a short woman by any means, but he towered above her and she realized for the first time she didn't even reach the center of his chest.

"And why not?" she demanded.

"I will not stand around and let this thief put his hands on you."

"Do you not trust me?"

His chest heaved as he stared down at her. "Of course I do."

"Then trust me on this. I can go in the city gates and plead to see Aladdin, beg him to spare my family if I agree to marry him." Ramsay's teeth ground together, so she hurried on with her plan. "With his attention focused on me, you can sneak in as planned and free the prisoners."

"And if he forces you to marry him? Uses a wish to ensorcell you into loving him?"

"He cannot," Safiyya spoke up. "An ifrit cannot create love where there is none. Aladdin will know this, I'm sure. Which means he will either woo her or make threats against her family. Either way, she still has to agree, which means she can stall."

Ramsay grunted. "I still don't like it, but I suppose we have no better options."

Hoping to soothe his worries, Victoria stepped in close and placed her hands on his chest. His pulse thumped beneath her touch in a tranquil rhythm she'd come to love after so many nights alongside him, sharing both his bedroll and his warmth.

"I know we can do this, Ramsay. Together. But we each have our own part to play. Trust me now the same way you did in the gnomish city."

The tension left his body and his shoulders sagged. He dropped his hands to her waist and drew her in against him while nuzzling his bearded face against her hair. "Be careful, wife. I don't want—no, I *can't* lose you. Not when it's taken so long to find you."

Lifting to her toes, Victoria pulled Ramsay down to her and kissed him, hard and fast. "You won't. Now get going, both of you. It should take half an hour to reach the throne room entrance. The other isn't too much farther."

After the two separated, Safiyya twisted Maziar's ring off her finger and passed it to Victoria. "Good luck, child, and thank you. I will never forget what you've done for me by bringing me so far."

"We'll get you back to your family, Safiyya. Keep Ramsay safe for me."

"I will."

She waited until they moved ahead with a second torch before she rubbed the ring. Maziar's colorful stream of mist poured from it and gathered into a physical form.

"I overheard much of the discussion between the three of you. It's quite the daring plan," the jinni said.

"It's the best I can do."

He bowed his head in an unexpected show of respect. "What is it you wish of me, Mistress Victoria? If it is within my power, it is yours."

"I wish for you to dress me in garments befitting a noblewoman seeking a husband. They must be the finest clothing you can muster, all silk from Liang and frost-roses from Eisland. I must become a creation of absolute beauty able to impress any monarch."

Maziar's lips turned up in a smile. "Very well then."

The jinni's magic surrounded her and tossed the hemline of her plain traveler's dress. A swirl of mysterious light spiraled around her from head to toe with stardust glimmers and golden fire that caressed with reassuring warmth. No matter how much the flames licked across her attire or danced over her skin, nothing burned, and by the end of it, her wardrobe had been transformed.

Victoria glanced down at the voluminous skirts then twisted from side to side. They danced and swayed with her, showing a hint of white petticoat peeking beneath the hem. As Maziar surveyed his work, he performed several flourishes of his hands. Little sizzles of magic popped around her at random intervals, although she couldn't see what he was doing until the miniature buds of several ivory roses appeared upon her bodice, drawing attention to her décolletage. Silver glittered on the petals like ice.

A mirror appeared on the passage wall, accompanied by additional torches. Victoria stared at the image of a woman she'd thought long gone, dead from society the day she left Creag Morden behind. Her dress was made of blue silk shot through with silver thread. Her hair no longer resembled a mess of straw, but shone with a lustrous golden glow, the long strands coiled upon her head with white frost roses.

"The best part is beneath the dress."

"*Maziar!*"

"What? I am referring to your weaponry, Mistress. Lift your skirts and look."

Hiking the heavy skirts of the dress revealed a garter-style sheath fastened to her slender thigh with the blade Griogair had given her tucked inside. The Gnome King's magical belt had been wrapped around the other thigh in the same fashion. They matched.

"Suitable?" Maziar asked.

"Yes." Her quiet voice trembled, so she cleared her throat and repeated herself with more confidence. "Yes, this is perfect, Maziar. Thank you."

"If I may make a suggestion?"

"Of course."

"I know you planned to ride into the city, but since time is a precious commodity you cannot waste, allow me to transport you and your steed to the gates."

She blinked, startled. It was the first time the jinni had ever offered aid without their request. "I thought you couldn't transport people."

"No, I said I could not relocate your large group across the kingdom at the time. Sending you and your horse a few paltry miles is nothing."

"Thank you, Maziar. I'd like that very—" Between one breath and the next, the dark tunnel blurred away and she blinked her eyes against the sunlight. Maziar was gone and she sat sidesaddle upon Rook within a familiar copse several hundred yards before Lorehaven's main gate.

"Much…" she finished in a whisper.

Victoria reached the city gates to find them manned by mercenaries bearing Liangese and Eislander features, and for the sake of her family, she played dumb.

Given no choice about whether she wanted to visit the palace or not, the hired thugs relieved her of Rook's reins and guided her to the palace instead.

Wherever she looked, anxious faces and skittish townspeople observed, a familiar groomsman among the first to greet her once she dismounted from Rook. As he accepted the reins from the guards, his eyes widened in recognition, followed by a fearful tremble. Victoria brushed a reassuring touch to his upper arm before she moved past with her unwanted entourage.

Despite her initial fears of reaching the palace to find wholesale slaughter and misery, Aladdin had not imprisoned everyone. She passed several faces from her youth, mostly servants and minor nobles who constantly lurked around the castle. They watched her with fear in their eyes, but not a single one of them stepped forward to speak to her. Not that she could blame most of them.

"I have only the utmost respect for you, my lord Aladdin." Victoria's steps faltered when she recognized her father's voice drifting from the throne room. "Our daughter would make a fine wife."

"Your daughter is not here," a stranger's voice replied.

"Ah, but she is headed this way. We received word two weeks prior of her intention to travel home. She should be on the road as we speak and to arrive any day."

A sour taste filled her mouth as she stepped into the long room. Her parents stood at the far end, close to the throne, where Aladdin had made himself comfortable beside an enormous tiger. From what she could see of him, he might have been considered handsome, if not for the devious smirk on his bearded face. He had intense eyes, and a lean body, his smooth chest exposed by an open black vest above low-fitting trousers. A fourth figure, with skin the rich color of pralines, hovered to the left of the throne. Unlike Maziar, the ifrit floated in the air with smokeless flames making up his lower half.

"Ifrit, go to the girl and ask her to come to me. Bring her here if she agrees."

"There is no need, Master. The girl is already here." He gestured toward the doorway and all eyes turned on Victoria.

"Mother? Father? What is going on?"

"Victoria!" Surprise filled her mother's voice. "Darling, we were speaking of you only a moment ago."

Yes. Speaking of selling me to a tyrant. She pushed the dark thoughts aside and forced a smile to her face before continuing down the carpet to the raised dais. At the end, she dipped into a curtsey and looked between her parents and Aladdin with feigned uncertainty.

"Where is Uncle Morgan? What's happening in the city? When I arrived, there was chaos everywhere and fires raging through the merchant quarter."

"Victoria, dear, there have been some changes in Lorehaven since you left." Her father stepped down and took her hand between his baby-soft palms. "This is Lord Aladdin. He now rules Lorehaven."

Aladdin rose from his throne and looked down at her from his higher position. Victoria dropped her gaze to the floor and curtsied again.

"Yes, she is as lovely as you said."

"Then you will accept our offer?" Victoria's father asked. "She will make you a fine, bidding wife, and we will do all in our power to assist you with your ascension."

"Yes, you have been most helpful so far. And with your new titles, you will be quite rich."

A nauseating sourness churned in her gut. Not only had her parents offered her as a stranger's plaything, but they had ingratiated themselves into Aladdin's good graces and sold out their countrymen.

"Thank you, my lord. We're honored by your esteem." Her father patted her hand then released her. "You'll be a queen, my dear. The Queen of Creag Morden. We're so proud of you."

"Take her to my room," Aladdin ordered his men. "I will be up shortly."

Visiting his room hadn't been part of her plan. She balked and dragged her feet when the same guards who had escorted her to the throne room took her by the elbow like chattel. "To your room? But we haven't yet been wed. It..." *Think, Victoria, think!* "It would be *improper!*"

When she threw their own words back at them, her father grimaced, and her mother shot her a dirty look. "But soon you will be wed, my dear. Your timing was impeccable as always. Isn't this fantastic? You may have missed your opportunity to marry Prince Joren, but now we've found a finer catch for you in our very own kingdom."

"She has a small point, my lord, as such things are not consummated until after a ceremony. Is it a deal?" her father persisted nervously. He fidgeted with his silver cufflinks.

"Yes, yes, it is a deal. You will remain in control of your estate, and I will marry this girl and become the rightful ruler of Creag Morden. A fair and just trade, I believe, for one so beautiful as her."

Perhaps this is my chance and the fates are smiling upon me, Victoria thought when light glinted over the golden lamp dangling from Aladdin's belt. *That must be it. I only need to take it from him.*

Playing the part of her former quieter and more timid self, she allowed the men to sweep her from the room and into the bedchamber once occupied by the king and queen. It had been transformed into a marvel of Liangese beauty, with no traces of Mordenian culture remaining.

And were the fate of the kingdom not at stake, she would have loved to explore and admire it all. Maybe one day, if she survived the encounter, she'd ask Ramsay to visit Cairn Ocland's southern neighbors with her.

Within minutes of her arrival, Aladdin stepped into the room. A few of his men lurked in the hallway, appearing greasy and unkempt, unlike their master. "I am not to be disturbed under any circumstance. If anything happens, deal with it yourselves," he growled before shutting the door behind him. He wasn't a huge man, his slight build contrasting Ramsay's enormous bulk, but he moved with a cat's agility and soundless grace.

"Are my parents safe?"

"Yes, and they will remain as such. I like to consider myself a man of my word. They were quite fortunate for you to return when you did, of course." He shrugged out of his vest and approached her, lamp still dangling from a tough leather cord looped around his belt. "Now it is time for us to become acquainted. Remove the dress."

Victoria scrambled back from him. "I will do no such thing." Remembering what Anastasia had told her about

Prince Edward's attack the night before their wedding, she prepared herself to fight not only for her life, but her pride as well.

"But you should, as soon you are to be my wife. Whatever I take from you now will be mine then—" He reached for her, his hand at the level of her breast, and the moment his fingers skimmed over the embroidered silk, Victoria cracked her fist into his jaw.

Aladdin stumbled back a step and blinked at her. "Ah, you are a feisty one, I see. Much like the women of my home country."

For a moment, Victoria forgot to play the role of the simple noblewoman. She stared at him. "I am?"

The false ruler rubbed his face before opening and closing his jaw a few times. She mourned that she hadn't broken anything and tensed her muscles, prepared for a fight. Or for him to call the ifrit to punish her for the transgression. "You are definitely the woman for me! We will celebrate and throw the grandest of weddings."

"We will?"

"I was told the women of this country were meek things, but you have proven otherwise." He lowered onto the pile of gigantic cushions on the floor, the mass of them an ideal substitute for a bed. "So then, wife-to-be, if we are not to consummate this new union, what would you suggest we do?" He patted his lap.

Victoria concealed her disgust behind a demure smile. "I

am an excellent storyteller…" Although she wouldn't have 1001 nights to distract him like Scheherazade in the old tale, she hoped to entertain her arrogant suitor for a single afternoon.

Chapter 15

USING A LITTLE of Safiyya's magic brought her and Ramsay to the first secret entrance in half the time Victoria had projected. The downfall, however, was that the dancing torchlight revealed her trembles had worsened, and what little color the sorceress had before they entered was now nonexistent.

She's dying. She may not endure this at all.

"A moment," she said, pausing to lean against the wall. A wheezing cough shuddered from her lungs.

Ramsay looked back on her with concern. "Perhaps you should wait here, Safiyya. No more magic. You've aided our cause enough, and what hasn't been done by sorcery, I'll do on my own."

"Yes, I think you are right," she said after another cough. "Victoria mentioned a spyhole. Can you see anything?"

Ramsay studied the wall with the eagle medallion, careful not to touch the wings.

"Try the eyes," Safiyya said. "They're glass."

Following her suggestion, he leaned in closer and peered through the small, tinted panes. A pale brown tinge colored everything in the room beyond, but it was who he saw that startled him. He almost didn't recognize Victoria in her fine clothes.

"Victoria is speaking with someone. Aladdin, I presume. A swarthy man with a long, thinly braided beard."

"Yes, that would be him. If Victoria is there already, then Maziar has aided her as promised. Go on ahead. Free the king while Aladdin is distracted. I will try and send word with my magic if something changes. And take these."

Ramsay accepted the gnomish hammer and a small clay disc from her trembling fingers. "What is it?"

"Crush it before you open the trapdoor. The spell will cloak you for a short time. For the next five minutes or so, no one will see, hear, smell, or perceive you in any way. Move quickly."

"I will. But shouldn't you keep this hammer?"

"Something tells me you'll be the one to need it."

A sinking feeling plunged Ramsay's belly toward his toes, something ominous about the old woman's words. "All right," he said, refusing to argue with her. "Then wait here in safety, Safiyya. We'll return soon with Samiran, and you'll be the one to have the honor of freeing him."

He took the last stretch at a jog, following the tunnel to its end. A short ladder was bolted into the wall, exactly as Victoria had described. He climbed up and slid open the latch before crushing Safiyya's spell in his fingers. The trapdoor opened downward, bringing a fine layer of dust with it. The dull fabric of a brown and gold rug sagged across the opening, but he pushed it aside and climbed into the empty larder.

Hoping five minutes would be enough time to reach the dungeons, Ramsay placed his trust in Safiyya's magic and rushed into the corridor. One of Aladdin's many mercenary guards patrolled the next hallway, an armed man with a scimitar in each hand.

While he could take him, something told him leaving a trail of bodies behind wouldn't be ideal to infiltrating the castle. Under no circumstance could he risk exposing Victoria.

True to Safiyya's word, he strode unnoticed past the mercenary and resumed his journey to the lower levels. Mordenian and Oclander castles couldn't be more different, the colors of her homeland dull and dismal, faded shades of gray and silver, and no stained glass. He passed a boring corridor with alcoves occupied by stone busts of her ancestors, the occasional painting, and another patrolling guard before reaching a descending path.

"Which way?" he muttered, staring at the two passages. Each one sloped downward, one curving to the left and the other to the right. As he debated which way to go, a plume of golden light flickered at the edge of the left corridor.

Ramsay hadn't seen a will-o'-wisp since his childhood, and spotting one in Creag Morden took him by surprise. He startled back a step and stared down the poorly lit corridor. The pins and needles feeling surrounding his entire body began to vanish by the time he made his way to the bottom, signaling he'd reached the end of Safiyya's spell.

The wisp had also vanished, but he no longer needed it. The smell alone told him he was in the right place, the stench of death and despair heavy in the air. A torch burned halfway down the corridor where two guards sat at a small table playing dice.

Ramsay drew his sword and charged, cleaving the first guard in half before either man knew what hit them. The surviving thief leapt back in an impressive acrobatic display and pulled twin daggers from his belt.

He brandished his weapons, spinning them too fast for even Ramsay to follow. If the display was meant to intimidate, it might have worked on a lesser man. Ramsay simply frowned, considered his chances, then took the most viable option available to him.

He shifted and charged forward on all fours. The startled thief faltered and fell back, fumbling his weapons in his attempt to scramble away from the massive bear.

Ramsay crushed the thief against the ground and bashed him into the stones, ending the scuffle and any noises of battle. For a moment he waited, fearful the fight might draw more guards, but no one came.

Once the coast was clear again, the bear shifter rose to two legs and continued down the corridor until he heard voices, the low murmurs of many people. The passage turned to the left and opened into a large room where several cells with barred gates lined two walls.

"Go away you Samaharan dog," a man spat from the first

cell. "We will tell you nothing."

Ramsay's brows shot up. "I only came to let you all out." He held up the keys and gave them a shake. "Which of you is King Morgan?"

An older man with a gray beard and silver-streaked hair limped up to the bars in the second cage. "I am he."

Ramsay stepped over and drew in a deep breath through his nose. He studied the man, looking down over his velvet doublet and curled-toe shoes. "You aren't the king. A noble, yes. An advisor perhaps."

"What makes you say that?"

Ramsay snorted. "Nothing about you resembles Anastasia." His expectations were of a great man, a powerful monarch willing to defeat a dragon for his child's safety. "You are too fragile and weak a human to have conceived the queen I know. I need the true king to step forward."

A second human emerged from the shadows and regarded him with solemn eyes. His clothes were equally as impressive, but he wore boots instead of the ridiculous velvet slippers. He filled out his doublet with broad shoulders and had the look of a former warrior.

"What do you know of my daughter? Who are you?"

"The man helping you escape," Ramsay replied, loathing the Mordenian tongue. He unlocked the cell door and swung it open wide. "Please trust me. I arrived with Victoria, and I am a loyal subject of your daughter. For now, you may call me Ramsay."

Ramsay recognized Queen Lorelei from Anastasia's description, dark-haired and lovely with a noble woman's poise. Her piercing blue eyes gleamed brighter than sapphire chips when she hurried to her husband's side and gripped his hand. "He isn't a danger to us. My magic may be bound by their ifrit, but I can sense Victoria's presence around him."

Eight people were more than Ramsay had expected to rescue. He looked over the assorted group, silently noting the injured and slowest among them. If they encountered resistance, he wasn't sure if he could save them all.

"Is there a closer entrance to your escape passage?"

The king's eyes widened. "How did you know about that?"

Ramsay grinned. "How do you think we snuck in?"

Queen Lorelei chuckled, a quick and brief sound. "Smart girl, our Victoria."

"She is," Ramsay agreed. "And right now, she is distracting Aladdin so you can escape your execution."

The two monarchs exchanged worried glances.

"What?" the shifter asked, filled with stomach-churning trepidation.

"My treasonous brother has flipped allegiances. Who you see in these cells are our most loyal followers and closest friends who couldn't bear to betray us."

"Victoria's parents have no such value on our lives, it seems," Queen Lorelei said sadly. "They have always envied us the throne, but when Anastasia became the Queen of Cairn Ocland, their jealousy worsened. They're waiting for our niece's arrival and mean to marry her to Aladdin."

"Then I will see you to safety and return for her. But first, we must sneak back to the larder unless you know a better way."

King Morgan shook his head. "No, the only entrances are the two Victoria knows of. Of course, after this, I may have to consider adding one down here on the lower levels. The crypts run along that wall there."

Ramsay jerked his head around. The wall the king had gestured toward was solid rock. "How far on the other side?"

"Huh? Oh, I don't know. Ten or twenty feet I suppose? It's all solid granite, I assure you. No prisoner could chisel his way out, even if they did know about the catacombs."

"One of you keep watch, I'll get us through."

After cracking his knuckles, Ramsay stepped up to the wall. The earth felt different in Creag Morden, but it still answered to his magic as he spread both palms over the cold stone. A moment of initial resistance passed, and then the unfamiliar rock yielded to his authority over it and the rough surface shifted apart, molding to his whims.

"What magic is this?" King Morgan asked in a whisper.

"It's beautiful," the queen said. "Look, he's tunneling through the stone."

"But when the thieves come down, they'll only follow us through," one of the prisoners said, the young man bearing a close resemblance to Morgan. He must have been one of the princes.

Ramsay gestured them all forward once he completed the opening. "Once I close it behind us, they'll never know how you escaped."

His tunnel met with the catacombs and the eight nobles hurried through. As promised, he sealed their escape route. King Morgan led the way through the twisting mausoleum pathways until they reached the main corridor. Ramsay looked up and down the passageway, trying to get a sense for where they were.

"The exit is this way," the queen told him, gesturing to the left.

"And the throne room entrance?"

"Back the other direction, but it's a long way to travel and would only lead us to danger. Why?"

"I left a friend there. No matter, I'll come back for her after I've seen you to safety, since we need to get Victoria next."

The queen laced her fingers together and closed her eyes. A faint wrinkle creased her brow. "I fear you won't find Aladdin an easy foe. He has a powerful magical being with him capable of hobbling even my magic. Although it kills no one, it summoned an endless supply of arms and weapons beyond the gates."

"An ifrit. Yes, I know. His name is Samiran and he's as much a prisoner as you were, bound to the lamp Aladdin carries. It was part of Victoria plans all along to confront Aladdin and steal the lamp back from him. He'll be powerless without it."

They rushed down a mile of torchlit corridor beneath

the palace until they reached a solid wall. Once King Morgan touched a plaque on the wall set in a shallow depression, the stone door rumbled to the side and revealed a small graveyard and tall mountains rising on the eastern horizon.

"Is there a safe place you can hide?"

"Here," Lorelei answered. She waved a hand around them. "We'll take shelter in one of the mausoleums, and there are supplies stored in the tunnels. Thank you for this, Ramsay. You have our gratitude, but… I fear we must ask more of you."

"If it's within my power, I'll try."

"Please, I know it is a lot to ask, but you must help my people," King Morgan said. "My youngest son, Stephen, was out with my most trusted guard when Aladdin struck. I believe they are hiding within the city, trapped."

"But Victoria—"

"Is safer in the castle than my people are in the city. Aladdin's men are cruel. Before he breached the castle, I witnessed my city on fire and my people terrorized. Please, if you can help them, I am begging you to do so. Please find my son and Sir Williford. One of the palace servants brought word to us of a resistance in the city. You must find and help them."

As much as he desired to run to Victoria's aid, he had to trust her to be a strong warrior capable of standing on her own. He just hated that she'd be standing on her own against a cutthroat thief with an ifrit at his command.

The Liangese mercenaries at the gate never stood a chance. Ramsay became a furry cannonball, all claws and teeth hurtling through them. He flattened one on impact and rose on his hind legs to rip the other in half.

According to King Morgan, most of the royal forces had been demolished in the initial siege or imprisoned in the city watch's jail when they stood up to Aladdin and refused to yield the throne. Burning oil and smoke sent black plumes into the air from siege machines brought to intimidate the resistance.

The scent of gunpowder filled the air, a smoky odor he'd only smelled once in his life, years ago when an adventurer from the south traveled through Cairn Ocland before their nation fell to Dalborough.

More dangerous as a bear than as a man, he bounded forward on a zigzagging pattern toward his target. Two hard pellets sank into Ramsay's broad shoulder, but the rest missed the mark and scattered to the air.

Shouts in their native language echoed across the city's entrance, no doubt calls for aid and a warning to their comrades. As his opponent tried to reload, the shifter landed in front of him, swiped with his claw, and tore the man down to the ground.

The queen thought her son and the final members of the resistance would be holding out at the temple devoted to Creag Morden's god.

Vivienne Savage

In theory, it gave him a location to focus his search, but the reality was that he didn't know their temples from any other building. Creag Morden's strange architecture bewildered him, every building on the street rising two to three stories tall. And the streets curved in odd directions and rounded back on themselves in circles instead of leading in sensible directions.

Traveling one deserted street after the next made him wonder how many had evacuated Lorehaven in the early stages of the invasion. As he bounded down a road into what he assumed was a residential district, he saw a sad face gazing back at him from a window, only for the expression to brighten and the eyes to grow wide with excitement before an adult yanked the child away.

There were families left after all, not gone and fled into the night, but trapped inside their homes.

"Now wait just a minute!" a loud voice protested down the next lane. "I'm only heading to the market to fetch milk for my son. His wet nurse hasn't come in days, and his mother is far too ill to produce."

"Right, and we're fairies here to sprinkle a little pixie dust," a second man taunted. "I think you're out looking for the resistance, if you ain't one of them trying to stir up trouble."

"I think he is too," a woman agreed. "Let's gut him."

Unwilling to let the mercenaries harm an innocent, Ramsay rushed around the corner and came upon a man and woman in black thieves' leathers holding a native Mordenian at blade point. They looked Liangese to him, with long dark hair fashioned into multiple braids.

A glance at their hands revealed them to be Twenty-Two and Five.

Excellent.

Ramsay grinned, baring his teeth before he raced in to the rescue. Their would-be victim saw him first, a chubby man with a smooth babyface. His scream—and possibly the thundering noise generated by a couple thousand pounds of bear—alerted them to Ramsay's approach.

Twenty-Two never had the chance to avoid him, struck so hard he flew into the adjacent brick building. Five dove out of the way in a spectacular acrobatic display while arming herself with a pair of metal fans. He turned to attack, but she spun out of his range and kicked him in the snout. A blade hidden on her boot sliced across his nose and drew blood.

As Ramsay roared and charged after the female thief, she plucked a crabapple-sized sphere from her belt and threw it on the ground. It exploded into a cloud of scarlet, burning mist, the heat of it in his eyes, in his nose, and filling his lungs. The red haze, along with his own tears, blinded him before a flurry of small cuts landed all over his body. Hard and merciless attacks punched him with small hand blades around his shoulders. He staggered back and swatted uselessly at the air while struggling to breathe.

He couldn't smell or see her, too overwhelmed by his discomfort to pinpoint her movements with sound.

Did she even make a sound?

227

Visible through his tears, her blurry silhouette flipped around over the paved road, but the next blink sent another flash wave of scorching heat beneath his eyelids. She kicked at him again and sliced open his chest. Thankfully, the shaggy, thick fur protected his throat to some extent.

"Don't just stand there!" someone cried from the left in the sweet and familiar brogue of a native Oclander. "Help him!"

"The bear is here to help! It's a shapeshifter!" another called in the same accent.

Metal clanged against metal, gifting Ramsay with a reprieve from the sprightly thief's assault.

Desperate to end the fight before the thief resorted to another trick, he slammed both of his forepaws against the ground and caused the street to buckle up and ripple down the road. It tossed several bodies up in the air, his enemy and the others who had come to his aid.

Struggling to see through the agonizing haze, he made out a wispy, female form sprawled on the ground and did the only thing he could under the circumstances—he rolled over onto her while praying he didn't also smush his would-be rescuers. Her scream cut short, silenced when his tremendous weight compressed the air from her lungs and flattened her defenseless body.

"That's one way to end it. Williford, get away before you're caught beneath him too, lad. I don't think he can see us."

Ramsay shifted to his human form and used his shirt to wipe his face. It didn't help.

"Ah, I thought so," one of the men said. "Haven't seen one of your kind in years, not since I was a wee lad."

Another pressed a cool bucket into his hands. "Here. You'll want to wash your face in cold water, and that's the best we've got. Their damned pepper bombs burn like the fires of hell, and the moment you use hot water, it's like your skin is peelin' off."

Ramsay knelt on the street and rinsed his face with a few handfuls of water before finally upending the entire bucket over his head. He regretted it. The tainted water seeped into every nick and cut that hadn't yet healed.

"Easy does it, lad. You're fine now. Already healing."

Ramsay blinked a few more times through his tears. Their blurry shapes came into focus, two bearded men in traditional kilts, the red and blue tartan pattern of an unfamiliar clan he'd never met. "You're Oclanders."

"Aye, or we were at least, before our mum moved us here to flee the Scourge years ago. We'd have moved back, but… this is home now." The bearded man gazed at a rising tower of black smoke in the distance. "And fightin' for it."

Tears continued streaming down Ramsay's face, but he resisted the urge to wipe his eyes. "So am I. My mate is a Mordenian, so this kingdom's trouble is my trouble now."

"I'm Errol," the larger one said. Silver strands laced through the broad-shouldered man's ginger beard. "And this is my little brother, Graeme."

"Pleasure's all mine. Always is grand to meet one of your

kind," Graeme said pleasantly.

"This is a nice conversation and all, but let's get out of the bloody street before more of the bastards come," a bald knight growled from behind them. He stood beside a young man with a baby face, peach fuzz above his upper lip, and a shiny sword with the royal emblem on the hilt. He recognized the eagle at once.

"You shouldn't be so rude, Williford," the young man said.

"No, he's right, lad. Lead on then."

With the others to lead him to the temple, they arrived in record time. Multiple levels constructed from pink and white marble towered above them with a high, pyramidal roof topped with a golden spire.

"None of the thieves have attacked the cathedral. I reckon it's because this Aladdin bloke has either respect or fear for the gods. So we've been bringing in those we can," the bald man said once they moved inside. Ramsay looked around at people huddled in the pews and against the far walls. Priests and priestesses moved through the crowd, tending to the wounded and passing out bread.

"Whatever his reasons, it's good to see folk out of harm's way." Ramsay swiped at his eyes a final time then turned to the knight. "If you're Williford, then you must be Prince Stephen."

"I am!" the boy exclaimed. "How did you know that, sir?"

"Your mother and father are safe. They send their love and asked me to come find you."

"What? But how?"

"It's a long story, but the quick and short of it is that Victoria led me in through the secret passage and I managed to free the prisoners in the dungeon. They're out safely, but asked me to find you. I'm to bring you to them."

Stephen stiffened. The boy stuck out his chin and straightened his shoulders despite failing to reach Ramsay's chest height. "I cannot leave while my people are in jeopardy, and I won't go until the last person is safe."

Ramsay stared at the boy with a mixture of grudging respect and exasperation. Every second in the city was a second away from Victoria's side. He had no idea where she was, how she fared, or what she was doing.

"Look, I can't get the entire city out, but I can ensure your safety at least. Once we deal with Aladdin and rid him of his magical slave, you can do whatever you like to help your people."

"I'm not going," Stephen repeated. "If you're going after Aladdin, I want to help."

"The lad's good with a sword," Errol said.

"Aye, and if you're planning on storming the castle, bear or not, you're going to need help," Graeme added.

"Looks like you've been outvoted," Williford said.

Ramsay looked from one resolute face to the next and decided not to argue further. He stood a better chance with help, and the boy—no, the *man*—deserved the chance to fight for his home. Stephen was as proud and brave as any Oclander.

"All right. Then here is what we're going to do."

Chapter 16

Twice during her story, Victoria had abandoned her seat and refilled Aladdin's wine, only for him to herd her back to his lap like a fluffy pet. The third time, she ignored his urging and took a seat on the cushions beside him, placing a plate filled with fruit and pastries on his lap instead.

"And that was what I have done with my life since leaving Creag Morden," Victoria concluded, weaving a masterful tale unlike any other. If she'd had a quill and paper, she could have penned a novel worthy of the book stores. *Maybe I'll survive to pen it. A Lady's Tale: Gone and Home Again.*

Aladdin lowered his palm to her knee. Her eyes darted down to it then to the golden lamp dangling by his left hip. "A fascinating tale. Perhaps I will not conquer this land of Cairn Ocland after all."

Victoria wet her mouth with a single grape, too cautious to risk tasting the wine and inebriating herself. "They're very powerful creatures, those shifters," she said without stammering. "Guarded and beloved by beings of spectacular ability. I'm told the fae aren't to be trifled with."

"Ah, my sweet, but I have something far more powerful than a fairy. I merely wonder if perhaps these beastmen would make better allies."

Victoria brushed his hand off her knee. "Oh? Well, it would be difficult to make friends with them if you put their queen's entire family to death."

"You wish me to spare that weakling king and his witch of a wife?"

"Queen Anastasia loves her parents dearly. She wouldn't ally her kingdom with yours if you executed them."

"Then it seems you have bought them another night. For now, I can think of far more enjoyable ways to pass the time than discussing your wretched uncle." He removed his heavy belt, lamp included, and tossed it to the silken cushions on the floor. When he returned his attention to Victoria, he leaned in closer and turned her face toward him with a rough palm cupped to her cheek. "What wonders lie beneath this fine dress?"

"You're out of wine," she said, leaping from her seat. Behind her, Aladdin chuckled.

"Maybe you are shy after all. A blushing virgin ripe for me to pluck."

"Perhaps a little more wine would help me relax," she replied. "But your bottle is empty."

"Then I will conjure another."

"No!" she cried as he twisted and reached for the lamp, quickly adding a nervous laugh to her outburst. "I would like it if you went and picked one for me yourself. So I can have a moment to prepare myself."

"Oh?"

"You see… I mean…" She ducked her head and twisted her fingers into her skirt. "A woman's first time should be special."

"Then I will procure the finest of wines and the sweetest pastries for your pleasure." He rose and wobbled on his feet, grinning down at her. "Do not move far, my lovely."

Aladdin stepped out of the room and Victoria didn't dare move until she was certain he had moved away. She thanked whatever stars and spirits were watching over her, for Aladdin had left his lamp behind. She lurched for the golden artifact, but ended up catching the hem of her skirt with her foot instead and tripping over the fabric. The cushions softened her fall at least, but it took a moment to untangle herself.

"Where did it go?"

The lamp had disappeared, swallowed by the sea of silk pillows. She tossed them aside one after the other until a golden glint caught her eye to her right.

"My sweet, I meant to ask—what is this?"

She froze at the sound of Aladdin's voice, her arm extended toward the uncovered lamp, fingers mere inches away from her prize.

"You treacherous snake."

Quicker than a cobra despite the vast amounts of wine coursing through his system—Victoria had lost track of how many glasses she'd refilled from the enormous decanter—Aladdin lunged forward to reclaim the lamp.

Victoria rubbed her fingers across the surface. "Samiran,

I wish—"

The bandit landed beside her among the cushions and grasped part of the lamp, initiating a desperate tug-of-war between them. "Samiran! Come at once from this lamp and capture her!"

A stream of golden fire poured from the mystical device and took the shape of a man. Samiran hovered nearby and tossed his head back to laugh. "I cannot, you fool. For as long as she also holds possession of the lamp, I am no longer able to do your bidding. I can grant no wishes or provide magic to either of you until a true owner is determined."

Aladdin and Victoria both scrambled to their feet while kicking aside cushions and pillows, but neither relinquished their tenuous hold on the lamp. "You don't know what you're doing, girl. Let the lamp go, and I will go easy on your punishment."

"No. This lamp belongs to Safiyya, and I promised to reclaim it." Her gaze darted to Samiran, a fleeting moment of eye contact held between her and the impassive ifrit. He said nothing.

"I know not of who you speak, but this lamp is mine. Release it!" Aladdin roared.

"Never."

Victoria took a chance and kicked out her left leg at Aladdin's knees, but the nimble thief twisted to the side and struck her with the back of his free hand. An explosion of pain danced across her cheek and rocked back her head, blurring

VIVIENNE SAVAGE

her vision with stinging tears. Victoria turned her face before the next blow connected, forcing his fist to skim past her jaw.

With a battle cry worthy of Griogair's approval, she shoved her body forward and threw all her weight into her opponent, taking him by surprise. They crashed to the floor and the lamp clattered away beyond their grip. Victoria tried to crawl forward, but Aladdin grabbed her ankle and yanked her back, tearing her skirts in the process. She kicked free and scrambled to her feet.

No time to fight him and tussle over the pillows. She needed the lamp firmly in her hands, and hers alone, if she wanted to defeat the ruthless thief.

"Someone trained you well, little one. Where did you learn to fight?" he asked.

"Does it matter where?" Victoria eyed him for weaknesses, positive he'd already studied her stance for the same. The dress. The stupid dress had become a burden to her now, outliving its purpose of getting her into a phony suitor's good graces by becoming a cumbersome obstruction. She ripped it, suddenly thankful for Maziar's salacious sense of humor.

I could call him, she thought, considering the ring on her finger, but then Safiyya and the jinni's warnings echoed through her mind. A jinni could not harm a human, nor touch the prison of another elemental.

And if she revealed its purpose to Aladdin and fell in battle, he'd have one more servant at his disposal. *No. Maziar must remain a secret.* As she inched toward the fallen lamp,

Aladdin did the same, keeping her in his sights.

"I become more impressed with you by the minute, girl. Come to me and I'll forgive this slight."

Victoria drew her knife. "No."

"Ah. So it comes to that, does it?" Aladdin did the same, his knife inches longer with a cruel, serrated edge. It gleamed in the light from the many candles flickering around the room.

Victoria's heart sank.

He feinted with the blade, testing her and going on the offensive. She weaved to the side and back, keeping on her toes each time he slashed through the air, but he left no openings for her to attack. Instead, the thief herded her away from the lamp like a lost sheep separated from the flock.

"I could do this all day," Aladdin boasted, chuckling at her as they danced back and forth across the carpeted floor. "But which of us will tire first? Give up, little girl. I don't want to damage my prize."

"No! This lamp belongs to my friend."

He laughed again. "A friend who could not be bothered to fight for it. Where is this friend?"

Couldn't be bothered? Safiyya had fought her way across multiple kingdoms, using her own life as the fuel to cross thousands of miles. Fury overtook Victoria and guided her hand—she lunged forward past Aladdin's superior defenses, catching him in the hand, in the thick meat of his thumb. Crimson flowed bright from the wound over the hilt of his weapon.

The thief swore and jerked his hand back. Suddenly presented the upper hand, Victoria went after him with the ferocity of a wolven huntress before he could have the chance to recover. Whether by skill or immense luck, her knife caught in one of the hooked edges on Aladdin's blade and ripped it out of his hand. The weapon went flying and clattered somewhere behind them both, far away from the lamp.

Yes!

If he wanted it, he'd have to abandon their fight. Victoria dashed toward the fallen lamp. Although she reached the ifrit's prison first, short-lived triumph ended when her agile opponent gave chase and tackled her the moment she closed her fingers around the gilded handle. Aladdin seized the lamp with one hand and yanked her head back with the other, gripping a handful of her hair in his bloody hand.

"You'll suffer for this disobedience. I will turn you into a proper and obedient wife if it's the last thing I do. Now, what do you have to say for yourself?"

Without releasing her hold on the lamp in her left hand, Victoria reversed her grip on the dagger in her right hand and plunged it backward into Aladdin's gut. It passed through his body without resistance. Hot blood spilled over her fingers as she ripped it upward toward his chest.

His other hand closed around her wrist and tried to wrench her away, too little too late to save himself. Victoria released the blade, raised her arm, and drove her elbow back into his face. His nose made a sickening crunch before he stumbled back away from her and collapsed on the floor.

With the lamp clutched firmly against her breasts, Victoria scurried away and whirled to face her opponent.

"I would have made you a queen," Aladdin gasped from the floor. "Everything in the world would have been ours."

"I don't need to be a queen to feel good about myself."

Aladdin's breath rattled in his chest and then faded away. He remained on the floor, motionless, the blood beneath him spreading out in an ever-widening puddle.

"You have done it."

Victoria jumped, startled by Samiran's voice. For a moment, she had forgotten the ifrit was outside the lamp.

"I didn't want to kill him," she whispered.

"He gave you no choice, and now the lamp is yours. What do you command of me?"

"Nothing. I meant what I said when I told him I'm here to return you to Safiyya. She has the tool needed to break you free from this thing, and I intend to keep my word."

Fighting their way through the city wasn't as difficult as Ramsay expected. Although they reached the most opposition when they neared the palace, a few trained mercenaries weren't enough to stand up against them. They encountered more of Aladdin's hired henchman than members of the thief gang, a blessing in disguise if the rest were anything like number Five.

Across Lorehaven, members of the city watch had gone

  Vivienne Savage

into hiding, biding their time until the opportune moment to attempt retaking the city. With Ramsay as a leader and Prince Stephen in his company, men surfaced in droves. Not only had the appearance of an enormous shapeshifter given them the upper hand, but he'd also bolstered their confidence.

"To arms, men!" Sir Williford shouted. "No matter what horrors this elemental sends after us, we will not fail to retake the palace!"

Ramsay could only pray Victoria had been successful in her attempt to reclaim the lamp. *Please,* he pleaded to the stars, and to any other entity willing to grant mercy. *Grant her whatever aid she needs.*

Brick and mortar exploded to Ramsay's right. On the palace steps, a pair of Liangese men knelt with a strange device and boxes of tindersticks. They aimed one of the immense tubes at the approaching squad.

"They have more explosives!" Prince Stephen cried. "Take cover!"

In his human body, Ramsay ducked behind a cart with the prince as the two mercenaries at the gate launched enormous, fist-sized artillery at their group. It soared past them and into the walled garden in the square opposite the palace, where it exploded and reduced several trees to wooden dust and splinters.

"They demolished most of my father's army in the initial attack," Stephen said. "We ordered our men to scatter their forces afterward."

"Good thinking. You'd have lost all of them otherwise." Explosives and magic relied on armies moving in compact groups or lines, removing dozens, if not hundreds, of men in one fell swoop.

"Aladdin's creature seems unwilling or unable to harm us. It turned my father's best knights to stone. Sir Williford is the last of them."

Another explosive soared past them and detonated to the left of the square. A man screamed.

"He's unable to take human lives unless threatened," Ramsay said. When he risked popping his head out from behind their hiding place, he saw his opening. They were reloading the tube, pouring in black gunpowder and packing it with a bamboo rod.

While crouching, Ramsay pressed both hands against the stone street. The earth responded beneath him as cobblestones reacted to his whims, his willpower coursing through each individual stone in a rippling effect until he reached the steps. He reshaped the stone and speared one artilleryman while tearing the ground out from beneath the second. The palace steps slanted and spilled the survivor onto his back.

Recognizing his shifter size would become a disadvantage in the castle, he remained human and drew his sword to lead the charge. He and Williford raced up the steps then shouldered open the palace doors.

"Take the upper levels!" Williford called to some of the guards behind them. "Where did you last see Aladdin?"

  VIVIENNE SAVAGE

"The throne room," Ramsay replied.

They met little opposition on their way to find Aladdin, but arrived to find an empty throne room.

"The hell?" Ramsay muttered. "They were all—"

A dart whistled through the air and landed in Sir Williford's neck. Several more struck Ramsay, sinking into his thigh, chest, and right shoulder. Heat throbbed from the points of insertion, and when he glanced to his left, he saw the knight staggering.

Three thieves in black stepped from behind marble pillars running parallel to the red carpet leading to the throne, each armed with a different weapon.

A man with a long, slender, black braid rushed Ramsay, a number two displayed on his cheek in red ink. His serrated blade threw up sparks when it crashed against the shifter's longsword. He remembered Safiyya's warnings about the thieves, and how their numbers reflected their rank among the notorious band.

These three had to be Aladdin's top fighters, and it showed in their prowess. Two kept Ramsay on his toes, dealing quick and efficient strikes without the wasteful flourishes displayed by the lower ranks.

To his left, Errol and Graeme faced off against a thief wielding a spiked mace on a long chain. Four kept them at bay by swirling the mace through the air and launching it toward them with swift kicks. Ramsay had to avoid the fast-striking projectile twice during his own fight. Each time he gained the advantage, his opponent steered him toward the whipping chain and vertigo spun the room around him.

He had to fight the poison in his veins.

"Williford's taken a hit!"

The knight fell to the floor, leaving Stephen to handle a skilled warrior with two scimitars. Through the sweat dripping into his eyes, Ramsay watched the prince desperately try to fend off the man's curved blades. Kept on the defensive, the young prince couldn't manage to get in a strike, and there was no one left to help him.

Except maybe Ramsay. Even though he'd be an enormous sitting duck for their attacks, he shifted in the cramped space and loosed an ear-splitting roar, but his opponent somersaulted backward multiple times to remain beyond the reach of Ramsay's massive paws. Right into the path of the flying mace. The distraction provided the time Errol needed to aim with his bow and arrow. The arrow sank into the neck of the thief menacing Stephen.

"Ha!" Ramsay said when he returned to his human form. "They aren't so—"

"Ramsay!" the prince yelled in warning.

He turned, twisting in time to avoid the spear hurled at his back, but too slow to block the axe coming down at him. He'd never seen the fourth man enter the room, but he may as well have been a ghost who appeared from thin air.

A blinding bolt of lightning blew Ramsay's assailant back a split second before the axe cleaved through his skull. Ramsay's hair stood on end and a line of fire burned across his ear and cheek, but he was better off than the charred corpse that hit the floor.

He turned and spotted Safiyya across the room standing in the opened passageway. The old sorceress wavered on her feet and dropped her hand to her side before slumping against the wall.

As a bear, Ramsay thundered toward the remaining thief where there were no pillars to inhibit his movement. He slapped the mace from the air with his paw, ignoring the pain as the jagged spikes ripped into his flesh. With the weapon no longer a threat, Graeme rushed in and drove his sword through the man's torso and Errol dragged Williford to cover. The knight's body left a bloody smear across the marble floor.

While the others tended to their wounded comrade, Ramsay transformed to his human shape and hurried to Safiyya. The sorceress had crumpled to the floor.

"Blasted woman, I told you no more magic," he said, kneeling beside her. "Safiyya? Safiyya, please, say something to me."

Stephen crouched beside him and laid a gentle hand on his shoulder. "I'm sorry about your friend."

A low growl rumbled in Ramsay's chest. "She's not dead yet. Williford?"

"He'll live, but we need to get him to a healer. Both of them."

"Then we need to cut off the head of the snake. We need

to kill Aladdin." Ramsay would tear the man limb from limb with his claws in Safiyya's honor. "Stay with her. I'll go after—"

Flames erupted to their left in a swirling pillar. Ramsay jerked Stephen to the floor then leaned across both the prince and Safiyya to shield them from the heat of what he thought had to be an attack, but no strike came. Victoria's scent filled his senses.

"Ramsay?" Nothing had ever sounded sweeter than his mate's voice. His attention jerked up from Safiyya's motionless body to the sight of his wife. Her dress had been torn, revealing most of her legs from the midthigh down, and the deep purple of a bruise splotched her cheek.

Rage overtook him, the force of his fury more powerful than any toxin in his veins. "Where is he?"

Hurrying to him, Victoria placed one hand over Ramsay's chest. "It's over. He can't hurt anyone anymore, because he's dead."

Fierce pride for his brave and beautiful wife swept through him. Ignoring the lamp she clutched in her other hand, he dragged her in close and squeezed her tight against him, but only for a moment. There would be time to celebrate later.

"We've retaken the castle, lass, but Safiyya is dying."

Ramsay's words struck her with the force of a hammer, while cold pins and needles spread over her body from head to toe. No, it couldn't be true. They couldn't have come this far

VIVIENNE SAVAGE

only to fail.

Her gaze snapped away from her husband to the motionless figure on the floor. Her younger cousin knelt there with Safiyya, a hand on her unmoving chest.

"I don't feel her breath," Stephen said. "I'm so sorry."

"No, she can't be dead," she whispered. Her hands trembled and the lamp nearly fell from her grip. "Samiran, what do we do?"

The ifrit streamed from his prison and gazed upon them with dimmed eyes. "Free me. Destroy the lamp with the hammer he carries, and perhaps it won't be too late after all."

Ramsay took the lamp from her numb fingers and set it on the floor. On the first strike from the gnomish hammer, an explosion of light blinded everyone, making them all turn away, and a powerful force swept through the room like a strong wind. Victoria's hair blew back from her face.

When her vision returned, the first thing she noticed were the disfigured remnants of the lamp strewn over the floor. Then her attention turned to Samiran. The freed ifrit knelt beside Safiyya with his head bowed and his hands held over her body.

Nothing happened.

"No…" Tears slid over her cheeks as she knelt beside the old woman. "Safiyya?" She whispered it at first, and with quivering fingers, touched her friend's motionless chest. "Safiyya, wake up. It's all over now, Aladdin's gone."

"She's gone, Goldi," Ramsay said in a gentle voice. He

 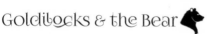

crouched behind her and set his hands on her shoulders.

"No, she can't be gone. It isn't fair. I promised her she'd live long enough to speak with him again." She looked across to Samiran. "Do something!"

"I've tried… of all of my gifts, restoring life to a mortal is not one of them," Samiran said. The ifrit lowered his head, features concealed by his full mane of black hair. "She's beyond the touch of my powers now, her life's spark too diminished. This is the most insidious killer of all. Human mortality and old age."

The tears continued to fall freely, no matter her effort to control them. Her throat tightened again, and a sob shook her shoulders. "It isn't fair. There has to be something you can do."

Samiran remained silent and the first stirrings of anger bloomed in Victoria's heart.

"All our time together, the one thing she wanted most was to free you," she snapped at the ifrit. "She used up everything she had to prolong her life and find you, even when, for years, she thought you abandoned her and your son."

Flames flashed around Samiran and his dark hair lifted from his shoulders, moving like tendrils of dark flames. His voice boomed, sending the others in the room scurrying away. "Do you think this is what I desire, mortal? No. I *loved* Safiyya more than my own life." He growled, the noise rumbling from him as feral as what Victoria would have expected of a shifter from Cairn Ocland.

Stephen stumbled back a step, but Ramsay moved in front

  Vivienne Savage

of Victoria. She brushed her husband aside, unintimidated by the ifrit's might.

"Then why did you leave her?"

Samiran silenced, and those flames of righteous anger diminished. "I didn't mean to," he said in a softer voice. "When our child was born, I wanted to honor the gift she had given me by presenting her a gift of my own."

"A gift?"

"A book she desired," Samiran murmured. "A rare book possessed by a sorcerer from another land."

"The Liangese wizard who captured you."

"Yes." Samiran stroked his fingers across Safiyya's wrinkled cheek. "My arrogance cost me everything I held dear. I believed I could trick him out of a prized possession, but I was the idiot who lost the game."

"Is there nothing we can do?" Ramsay asked.

"There is one thing," Samiran said in a quiet, defeated voice. "But I fear if I do it, she may never forgive me."

Victoria scrubbed her cheeks with the back of her hands and tried to rein her sniffles under control. "What thing?"

"Give my life and all that I am to feed the mere spark of her that remains in this body."

"If you did that… her entire journey to free you would be in vain."

"Yes," the ifrit said. "Now I war with myself over whether I should respect her final wishes or fulfill my own. Tell me, mortal, what should I do?"

"You should…" The words died in her throat before she could utter a command for him to restore Safiyya to life. "I can't tell you that. If it were me, I know what I would want. I would want Ramsay to live."

Ramsay dropped his chin and let his powerful shoulders sink. "And if it were my choice, I would tell you to hell with her desires, even though I know it's wrong." A heavy silence followed before Ramsay closed his eyes. "I would do it, because there is no greater reason for a sacrifice than love."

Hot tears slipped down Victoria's cheeks and blurred her vision as she set a sympathetic hand on Samiran's shoulder. The ifrit felt warm and alive, like any human man beneath her fingers. She squeezed and gazed into his smoldering gold and red eyes. "Ignore what we would do, and do what your heart tells you is right."

"My heart tells me she has suffered long enough and deserves more than death so far from her home and family," he whispered as he gathered Safiyya's limp body up in his arms. "All my life, in so many millennia, I never knew I could love anyone so much. My older sister hated Safiyya from the first moment she realized I had fallen for her. She called me the desert's greatest fool and said I would come to regret my decisions one day, once I experienced the frailty of mortal life."

Without glancing up at them, the ifrit squeezed Safiyya tighter and kissed her temple while his shoulders shook with raw, unfettered emotion. "I do not regret a thing, Safiyya. Not a day alongside you. Not a day of hoping to see you again."

A tight, hard lump in her throat kept Victoria from speaking. Witnessing the love and raw pain in Samiran's eyes struck a chord deep within her soul. She couldn't imagine losing Ramsay.

Her bear took her by the hand and squeezed, renewing her pain with a fresh wave of tears as she mourned the fate of the two lovers before them. Why hadn't she told Safiyya to remain in safety outside the city?

Samiran looked up and met her gaze. "This is not your doing, but I would ask you one thing."

"Anything," she said, unable to hold back a sob.

"Please tell Safiyya that my only wish, if I could grant one to myself, is that she and our son can one day forgive me."

"I will."

He closed his eyes and dropped his head down. "All that I am will be yours, Safiyya." And without another word of apology, he kissed the old woman's pale, wrinkled lips. Even though the life had already left her, Samiran appeared to breathe it into her frail body anew.

Victoria wanted to stop him, but the words died in her throat and her heavy tongue refused to move. Numbed by his sacrifice, she watched the ifrit funnel his essence into Safiyya's motionless body. Soon they were as bright as a golden bonfire, surrounded by the flames of his elemental magic. A column of energy rose higher and higher as flames licked the ceiling and left scorch marks against the stone before swelling to reach a cataclysmic crescendo. Ramsay's arms closed around Victoria and spun her away from the magical effects.

He didn't release her until the light faded away.

"What happened?" Graeme called over.

Nothing remained of Samiran and Safiyya but smoldering embers drifting to the ground. Eventually, even those faded.

"They're gone," Ramsay breathed.

"But… he was supposed to save her," Victoria whispered, panic clawing its way up her throat. "Where is she? How do we know it worked?"

Ramsay slipped his arm around her waist and drew her close. "We have to trust that Samiran delivered her home."

"But… but we didn't get to say goodbye. We didn't get to tell her what happened." The pressure in her chest continued to build, until Ramsay brought her head to his shoulder and the first wracking sobs tore out of her.

"I know, lass. I know," he said, smoothing his hand down her hair in an effort to comfort her.

"Why does it hurt so bad?"

"Because Safiyya was a friend," he murmured against her hair. "Because she—" Ramsay jerked back and gasped, and because nothing ever scared her bear or drew that much of a reaction from him, Victoria lifted her cheek away from his chest and whirled.

Those same glowing embers had multiplied into a radiant cloud of gold and indigo, creating rainbow colors that swirled like a cosmic force. It was as if the stars themselves had materialized in the room.

  Vivienne Savage

Each speck and particle drew inward, slamming soundlessly together and sweeping warmth throughout the room.

Samiran had returned, although he now stood beside a woman with waist-length black hair and eyes of the deepest, most beautiful violet Victoria had ever seen. She wore an emerald, midriff-baring top fitted against her upper body and a trailing skirt stitched with gold trim and colorful flowers.

Safiyya looked exactly as Victoria would have imagined her to appear in her youth, as elegant and beautiful in vision as she had been in spirit.

"I... I am alive," Samiran breathed, appearing both bewildered and confused. He turned to face Safiyya. She took both of his hands and gazed up at him with tears shining in her eyes. "So are you. I do not understand. I performed the sacrifice. I gave my essence to you."

"You did, little brother," a melodic voice spoke from the empty air, seeming to have no source while echoing from all directions at once.

A woman of indefinable beauty appeared in an explosion of smokeless flame. Magic radiated from her in pulsing waves of mystic essence, and each miniature burst tickled static across Victoria's skin. The nameless woman's eyes burned like fire in a flawless face. Most lovely were her robes, violet, gold, and crimson. Although her feet didn't touch the ground, the floor beneath her bare soles smoldered while she hovered above it.

"Yasmina," Samiran whispered. He tugged Safiyya behind

him and put himself between all of them and the ifrit queen.

"Be at ease, brother. I have not come to harm or cause strife. In fact, I came to ensure your beloved wife succeeded in her task."

"You?" Ramsay said. "You're the flame that led me to the dungeon."

"And in the gnome city too, remember?" Victoria added. "I thought I saw a flame flickering where we found the hammer."

"Yes," Yasmina said. "Like your fairy godmothers, I could not interfere directly. Such is the way of magic and beings who bear our vast responsibilities."

Safiyya stepped up beside Samiran then gazed at her unblemished hands. "How is this possible?"

"Samiran gave you all that he was. His life. His magic. His very soul. A mortal body cannot sustain such power, not even an enchantress of your caliber. So you have become more."

"But I should not be here," Samiran said.

Yasmina turned her vibrant gaze on her brother and smiled. "I did not come this far to see you give up your life. What you gave, I returned in part, but only after Safiyya made her transformation. After all, it would not do for either of you to outlive the other."

"What are you saying?" Victoria asked.

"I've been made into a jinni," Safiyya whispered.

"Yes," Yasmina said. "As has my brother. He no longer possesses the full strength of an ifrit, having given half of it to you, but I do not believe he will complain about the sacrifice."

"I would have given my life," Samiran said. "Losing my powers means little, not with what I have gained."

The tightness in Victoria's throat eased and tears sprang to her eyes, this time born of joy. "Thank you for helping them. For helping all of us."

Yasmina bowed her head, then turned her gaze on the ring Victoria wore. "As for Maziar…"

"Oh, please," Victoria said, stepping forward and holding out her clasped hands. "Please free him, Queen Yasmina. I don't know his past crimes, but he's helped us of his own free will. We never would have saved Samiran without him."

"Peace, child. Maziar has served his punishment long enough and shall be freed, as you promised him. Since Samiran no longer holds such power, I will honor the agreement in his stead."

When the queen snapped her fingers, Maziar streamed out from the ring in a long plume of turquoise fire. Victoria heard his laughter and a quiet whisper of thanks as the freed jinni vanished through the castle walls into the open sky beyond. The ring remained on her finger, transformed from an enormous ruby to a milky white opal instead.

"Do you think he'll be good?" Victoria asked.

"We can only hope so," Safiyya replied. "But I believe he will. And maybe, one day, when he has enjoyed his freedom, he will return to the Opal Spire and meet the rest of his family."

"Family?"

Safiyya turned to Samiran and took both of his hands,

 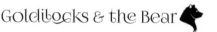

beaming up at him. Her violet eyes twinkled with mischief. "There are so many things to show you, my love."

Yasmina turned her attention away from the reunited couple and focused on Victoria next. "And what of you?"

Victoria faltered, feeling like a doe caught in a hunter's sights. "Me, Your Highness?"

"Yes, what wish may I grant you for all you have done? What desire can I make yours?"

Before her mind could contemplate the depth of what Yasmina had offered, an answer flew from Victoria's lips. "My only wish is for Lorehaven and all the towns ruined by Aladdin's men to be returned to how they were. I know—" Her throat tightened and she swallowed back the thick lump. "I know you cannot return those he killed, but I wish for you to fix the rest of the damage. Restore our cities and these broken homes. Return the treasures stolen and looted gold where they belong."

"A selfless wish, one I will gladly grant. It is done."

Victoria blinked. "Already?"

"Indeed." Yasmina smiled and drifted away. "And as a final gift, when you are ready to return home with your companion, your belt will take you wherever you desire. All the stones have been recharged."

Victoria dropped her awed gaze to the band around her thigh. Each sapphire and diamond shone with an inner light, miniature blue stars twinkling more brightly than they had before.

VIVIENNE SAVAGE

"Thank you."

In a flash, Yasmina became a radiant, burning ball of flame that danced through the air, sweeping magic through the room and removing the corpses of the deceased thieves. Samiran and Safiyya adopted similar forms.

"Thank you," the two lovers spoke together as their twin flames circled around Ramsay and Victoria. "If you should ever need us, lovely Victoria, remember our names. We will not forget what you've done here for us."

"Goodbye," she whispered as Ramsay held her close. "I won't forget you either."

In the next breath, they were gone.

At some point during the various magical occurrences, the survivors' wounds had been healed as if they'd never occurred. Victoria only wished she could thank Queen Yasmina yet again for her assistance. She and Ramsay left Stephen and Sir Williford in the throne room with the two Oclanders, and then they hurried outside. As promised, there wasn't a single stone out of place in Lorehaven's city streets. Victoria gazed around in wonder at the transformation alongside bewildered citizens staring at their surroundings in awe.

"It was magic," someone said. "A great flame swept over the city, and I thought it was the end, but it did not burn. As it passed, everything was made whole."

"Who could have done such a thing?" another asked.

"It was the Queen of the Ifrit," Victoria called out. With Ramsay's hand to balance her, she climbed up on a low wall and looked out over the people. "By her kindness, Aladdin's destruction has been undone."

"Will he be back?" a woman called out.

Victoria shook her head. "No. Aladdin and his thieves are dead. King Morgan and Queen Lorelei are safe. Prince Stephen holds the throne room in his care until they can return to the city."

"Where are they?"

Before Victoria could answer, a loud whooshing sound swept over the city and a large shadow passed overhead. Amidst instinctive cries of fear, a few citizens shouted out in relief upon recognizing the three riders on the dragon's back.

"It's Queen Anastasia!" A young boy whooped and threw his hands in the air. "Look, Mum, Queen Anastasia! And that's King Morgan behind her."

Victoria hopped down as Alistair landed in the city square. She rushed into her cousin's arms the moment Ana slid from her husband's back.

"We only received word a few hours ago and came as quickly as we could," Ana said, squeezing her tight. "Alistair spotted Mother and Father as we flew over the forest, or we would have been here sooner. What happened?"

A laugh bubbled up in Victoria's throat, mixed with a relieved sob. She hugged Ana closer and looked past her shoulder to her aunt and uncle. Ramsay helped them down from Alistair's back.

"I'm not sure you would believe me if I told you," she said, pulling back. "But we're safe now. Lorehaven is free of Aladdin's tyranny."

King Morgan stepped over, staring at the city. "But how is this possible? We saw the fires and heard the battles before we were locked away."

"I sense a strange magic," Lorelei murmured. "Much like the spirit Aladdin controlled, but more powerful."

"It was Yasmina, Queen of the Ifrit," Victoria told them. "After we defeated Aladdin, she returned the city to rights as a gift for helping her brother."

"Aye, lass, because you asked it of her." Ramsay stepped up to her side. "Don't give her all the credit. *You* defeated Aladdin, not Yasmina. Victoria was granted a single wish by a... by a demi-goddess, and all she asked was for your cities to be restored."

Lorelei stepped forward and pulled Victoria into her embrace, and then she kissed each of her cheeks. "Thank you, my dear. And thank *you*, Ramsay. Had it not been for your help, we would have been led to our deaths."

"So...basically what you're saying is, there's nothing here for me to do." Ana set her hands to her hips and stared at them all, a smile tugging at the corners of her mouth.

"Well... some of the families will need help, I'm sure. Yasmina can't return the dead or soothe emotional damage. People have lost loved ones, and women were taken from their homes to join his harem."

Ana's smiled dimmed. "Of course. We will do whatever we can to see everyone is compensated and taken care of."

"I will do whatever I can as well," Ramsay offered. "Where do we start?"

King Morgan gazed into the distance while stroking his chin. "Though it pains me to say it, I now have the dishonor of dealing with my rather ignoble brother and sister-in-law."

"What will you do with them?" Victoria asked in a quiet voice.

Morgan's stern expression softened. "I'm not so heartless as to put them to death, though they would have happily seen my head chopped off. But I believe they no longer have a place here in Creag Morden."

"Nor Cairn Ocland," Anastasia added.

"Therefore, I believe it best if I banish them to your mother's home kingdom, Victoria. They will be stripped of their titles, which shall of course, be passed down to you. You, Victoria, will always have a place here."

The cold, hard knot in her stomach loosened. "I think that's more than fair, Uncle."

"Do you want to be there when I pass sentence?"

Victoria shook her head. "No. I have nothing left to say to them. Only…that I wish them a safe journey." Although they'd hurt her with their immeasurable cruelty, they were still her parents, and she had no desire for harm to befall them.

"So it shall be."

Epilogue

L OOKING BACK ON her first adventure, Victoria couldn't help but marvel at everything she had done. She didn't feel like the same woman anymore after battling bandits and trolls, befriending elementals, and accepting the titles once belonging to her parents. Whether she ever returned to Creag Morden or not, she was now Duchess Summersfield.

After recuperating in Lorehaven for a few days, she and Ramsay had used the belt to return to Castle TalDrach, much to Anastasia's bewildered amusement. She hadn't understood the need to deplete the magical item when they could all fly back, but Victoria had simply shrugged and said she wanted to be home sooner rather than later.

Ramsay's fear of heights would be a secret she took to her grave.

They had another night to themselves in Benthwaite before Ana and Alistair returned. A night devoted completely to one another.

"I need to return to Clan Ardal," Ramsay told her the next morning as they lay in bed. "I've been gone far too long."

"I know," she whispered, trailing her fingers through the soft curls on his chest. "How soon do we need to leave?"

"I should start back today, but you don't have to rush." He placed his fingers over her lips when she lifted her head. "Get your things in order here first, lass. This was your home, and surely there are things you'll want to bring. People you'll want to spend time with. I'll return in a week or two after I've ensured the clan is settled. With Heldreth and Talbot still in Etherling, I can only imagine the work that's piled up."

"I understand. I… do you think they'll accept me?"

He rolled her to her back and leaned over her, one hand cupped against her cheek. "I can't believe in anyone not loving or accepting you," he said. "But even if they didn't, I wouldn't care. I'd renounce my title and retire happily with you to wherever you chose. Even if it was in Creag Morden."

"Ramsay—"

He silenced her with a kiss, and then he gave her something else to focus on, making love to her with the tenderness missing from their previous passionate and wild couplings. When she woke again, hours later, Ramsay was gone. She buried her face against his pillow, breathing in his scent, and wondered how she'd endure during the time apart from him.

After their shared experiences on the road and their blissful nights of recovery, even one day seemed like it would be forever.

Had this been how Safiyya and Samiran felt during their time apart? If so, she didn't know how her friend had survived. Sadness placed a leaden weight upon her chest and left a soul-deep ache where her husband belonged.

"Do I love him?" she wondered aloud to the empty room. "Is it possible to love a man after knowing him for so little time?"

At the time of his request to court her, their match had felt sensible, forged by friendship, respect, and even passion, but she'd never considered love to be part of the equation. Becoming his mate had been driven by her affection and hope for more in the future. Now, it seemed that future had come sooner than expected.

He promised to return soon. He'll be back, and I can tell him what's in my heart.

A knock drew her from the bed, but she didn't make it halfway across the room before the door opened and her cousin's ginger-haired daughter bounced inside.

"Victoria, Victoria, look!" Elspeth called.

"Elspeth, you shouldn't barge in rooms without permission," she chastised, though there was little heat in her words. The truth was she was glad for the distraction.

"Sorry," the girl apologized, her excitement dimming. She bit her lip and looked down at her feet, leaving Victoria feeling heartless.

"It's all right, my sweet. Come here, show me what you have."

The light returned to Elspeth's gold and blue eyes. She bounced up and down on her toes, a ball of endless energy clutching something in her small hand. A bit of the black cord escaped her clenched fist. "It's the very best thing," she said, opening her palm to reveal the glossy pendant. "See? It's a bear! Like your husband."

"I do see, and it's beautiful." She picked up the necklace and admired the carved stone figure. The gem flashed in a hundred different colors, as though fires and rainbows burst beneath the surface.

"I found it in the courtyard," Elspeth said, "and I want you to have it."

"But this is an expensive gift, little one, and surely belongs to someone."

"Nuh-uh," the girl disagreed. "Mummy asked all around and it doesn't belong to anyone, so she said I could keep it, but I want you to have it."

"You don't want it for yourself?"

Red curls bounced in the girl's face when she shook her head. "It's for you," she insisted.

Victoria knelt and hugged the girl tight. "Thank you. I'll treasure it always."

"Is it prettier than the things you found in the lost city?" Elspeth asked. The girl had been enthralled by the story of the gnomish kingdom.

"Much prettier," Victoria told her. "Especially because it came from you."

Elspeth beamed at her. "When I grow up, I want to explore it and solve the mystery. I'm not afraid of stinky old trolls."

Victoria laughed, amused to no end by her younger cousin's proud posture. "You know what? I believe you. One

  VIVIENNE SAVAGE

day we'll go back and find out what happened. Your mother wants to see it for herself."

"Okay, but I'm going to be the one who discovers the secret!" Elspeth kissed Victoria's cheek and ran out as fast as she'd arrived.

The next two days passed more slowly than watching paint dry on canvas. She tried to keep herself busy with the children and her packing, but every morning she checked her belt in the hopes that the stones would be fully recharged.

She didn't want to wait two weeks for him to come fetch her. She'd go to him as soon as the magic allowed her.

Too restless to remain indoors, Victoria headed outside into the afternoon sunlight. The orchard beckoned, so she grabbed one of the baskets piled beneath the trees and set to work plucking sweet apples and fuzzy peaches from the branches. Thanks to the magic that clung to the castle, the trees bore fruit all year, no matter the season.

"How did I ever deserve such a beautiful woman?"

The sound of Ramsay's voice behind her made Victoria's heart skip a beat and her breath catch in her chest. She spun around, certain her imagination was playing tricks, but her gaze focused on the man standing only a few yards away. The basket handle slipped from Victoria's hand. Her bounty of fruit hit the grass, and a couple bounced free over the wicker edge.

"You're here."

"I am. You see, I realized something as I was traveling, and it couldn't wait."

Goldilocks & the Bear

Her feet finally cooperated with her brain. She dashed across the orchard toward him and into his waiting arms. Chuckling merrily, he caught and spun her in a circle.

"What did you realize?" she asked once her feet touched the ground again.

"That you mean too much to me to be left behind with promises. When we leave this castle, it'll be together. The bears aren't the ones who need me right now, and I won't be that mate who leaves his new bride alone."

"You can't do that, Ramsay. The others are still in Ether—"

"I met Heldreth on the road coming back here. A funny thing happened in Etherling a day ago. It seems suddenly all the overgrowth burned away all at once. Incinerated by an invisible force."

Her breath caught in her throat until she finally uttered, "The jinn."

"Aye, that was my thought after she told me what happened. They didn't appear to take credit for it, but their aid was sorely needed. Talbot has remained behind to perform the remainder of the stonecrafting that is needed, and Heldreth will be returning to our clan. My place is here with you."

Victoria melted against him as they kissed. Ramsay's arms around her swept away the sadness that had been plaguing her since his departure and made her all the more certain of her feelings. Somewhere on the road, between all their bickering and their lives being threatened, between her growing respect and her fond affection, she had fallen head over heels in love with her husband.

"I love you," she said when they broke apart.

Ramsay's eyes widened. "Say that again, Goldilocks."

"I love you, and we don't have to stay here. I'm ready to go home with you to Clan Ardal. Today. Now if you like." The words continued to rush out of her. "I was waiting for the belt to charge, and then I was going to come to you, because I couldn't stand you not knowing how I felt. And I hope one day you can love me as much."

Ramsay took her face between his hands, his palms warm, his calloused thumbs smoothing over her cheeks. "Lass, I've loved you since you drew a dagger on me. I might not have realized it then, but I admired your spirit and your bravery from the first moment we met."

"You did?"

"I still do. My only regret is that I didn't tell you sooner."

"Say it," she whispered, loving the way he grinned down at her.

"I love you."

"Say it again," she pressed.

"I love—"

Victoria surged forward and kissed him, knocking them both to the ground. They rolled across the grass and came up for air, laughing. For a time, she was content to remain stretched out at his side, wrapped in his arms, while they both enjoyed simply being together. After a while had passed of cuddling beneath the cloudy sky, Ramsay helped her to her feet and brushed off her clothes and hair.

"What's that charm?" Ramsay tapped his index finger against the pendant she wore. It dangled from a thin black cord. "I've never seen you wear it before."

"Oh this?" Victoria raised the bear-shaped piece of black opal between her thumb and index finger. "Elspeth gave it to me after you left. She said she found it while playing in the castle courtyard, and she thought I'd like to have it to remind me of you while you're away."

"It's quite handsome."

Victoria smiled. "It is," she agreed. Each faceted edge of the bear carving reflected a different color. It felt warm beneath her touch, her lucky charm she'd worn in the bath and even to bed since Elspeth gave it to her.

The trinket reminded her of him and made it feel as if he were always near. She rubbed her fingers over the glossy gemstone and imagined running as a bear like her husband. And their future children.

As the fleeting thought whispered through her mind, Victoria's knees buckled and her weight shifted.

She toppled back onto her behind, a painless landing in the soft grass.

"Victoria!"

She stared in shock at her own hands—or paws, as it were. Fur the color of pale cream gleamed under the sunlight, shining gold and white with large ivory claws. She opened her mouth to speak but a low rumble came out instead.

Sweet stars, what's happened to me? I'm...I'm a bear! But no, I'm human. I want to be myself again!

With the single thought, she experienced the same odd sensation again, but in reverse. Fur and claws gave way to smooth skin and unpainted nails, and she gasped in a startled breath.

"What happened?"

"You became a bear." Ramsay crouched beside her and touched her cheek. "The most beautiful bear I've ever seen."

"But how?"

His eyes remained wide with wonder. "I have no idea. You were touching your pendant and had the most wistful look on your face."

"I was thinking about you," she whispered. "How I wished to know what it would be like to run with you and our children one day."

"Children?" A warm grin lit up his face.

"*One* day," she stressed, the panic at her sudden transformation fading away and leaving wonder in its place. "Look, I still have my clothes on."

"You do."

"But it takes your kind years of mastery to manage it."

"It does."

She lifted the pendant in her palm and gazed at it. Giddy joy filled her, a warm rush conveying a silent message blossoming from her heart. "It's Yasmina's gift to me," she whispered. "She wanted me to have something for myself. For... for us." *I wish to be a bear.*

For the second time, her body transitioned into the larger shape. Her vision sharpened, and the scent of the orchard filled her black nose with the fresh aroma of clean grass, fragrant flowers, and fruit. She rolled to her feet and tested her new body, her laughter coming out as a soft chuff as she spun about in place. Suddenly Ramsay was beside her, larger still, his caramel-colored fur shining like bronze in the sunlight. He nuzzled his snout to hers and rumbled in affection.

It was the perfect ending to the story she'd have to write one day. Goldilocks and her bear, she thought. It had a nice ring to it. More importantly, it had a happily ever after, and as far as Victoria was concerned, that made any adventure worth the effort.

About the Author

Vivienne Savage is a resident of a small town in rural Texas. Over a cup of tea, she concocts sexy ways for shapeshifters and humans to find their match.

To get on Vivienne's mailing list for news and upates, go online and visit http://viviennesavage.com/newsletter

Vivienne's Facebook: https://www.facebook.com/Savage.Books/

Website: http://www.viviennesavage.com/